the Jewel Carriers

A Novel by
Charles Edward Varney

Based upon the true story
of Abdullah F. Akbar.

Published by Creative Ink
Balboa Island, California, U.S.A.
All rights reserved.

Library of Congress Number—99-96249

ISBN: 0-9676744-0-9

Creative Ink

P.O. Box 5406
Balboa Island, CA 92662
www.thejewelcarriers.com

DEDICATION

To Bob — Enjoy — it's the real thing! Chuck V.

I dedicate this novel to the men and women, around the world, who gave their lives to resist the Soviet aggression in Afghanistan. May they rest in peace.

I wish to thank my wife, Diane, who stood beside me during this work. I would also like to thank Shirl Thomas and Barbara DeMarco Barrett, who helped me edit this book...to Mr. G. A. Ayeen for his expertise and wisdom. And, finally, to Michael Keeler and Paul Nicoletti, who were great friends and graciously gave me insight about the journey of life.

Charles Edward Varney

FOREWARD

IN THE NAME OF ALLAH—THE COMPASSIONATE AND MERCIFUL

In the name of Allah, the compassionate and merciful, I dedicate this book to the Mujahidin. These "Holy Warriors" fought and lost their lives in the Jehad—the "Holy War" against the barbaric Soviet invaders and their communist puppets.

We surely know that my compatriots' spirits are in paradise and, that the curse of Allah will be bestowed on those individuals, who used the cause of Jehad, for their personal and political gain. It is a given, that they know they will suffer a terrible life in this world, and hellfire awaits them, in the hereafter. We should applaud all those who worked for the cause of peace, and the nations who took action to stop discrimination and ethnic cleansing, similar to the atrocities in Bosnia and, more recently, in Kosovo.

Everyone should support a peaceful solution to the problem of the Palestinians' plight. We should condemn all kinds of aggression. We should strongly condemn the killing of thousands of civilians in Chechnya by barbarous forces of what was, at one time, a world superpower—The Evil Empire—humiliated and defeated in Afghanistan and reduced to the "laughing stock" of the world.

I thank Allah for saving my life countless times. My gratitude goes out to my mother, who compassionately prayed for me; to my father for making me the person I am today; and, finally, I would like to thank my partner, best friend, and dear wife, Laila, and of course, our wonderful children, Zubair, Neela and Medina, for their loving support.

Abdullah F. Akbar

CHAPTER 1

A Taste of Hell

I came to, lying face down in a pool of blood and water on a cold slab floor.

I'm dead.

Silence enveloped me.

I struggled to raise my head. Everything loomed dark except for a bright halo of light directly in front of me. It appeared to come from a lit doorway.

Praise Allah! I'm alive.

I remembered what happened. I had retreated from the dawn attack on the Afghan regime's ammo fort, when a Soviet helicopter's missile landed right behind me and catapulted my body into the air.

Now, a faint silhouette of a man approached slowly from the glaring doorway.

He broke the silence. "He's OK! He's OK!"

My brief elation immediately changed as my whole body froze rigid.

I didn't recognize the voice.

Think, Abdul. Afghan—but definitely not one of our freedom fighters. My god, I didn't make it. I've been captured by the damn communist regime.

Blood and mud caked around my eyes as I strained to make out my surroundings. To my right, a window framed the low-lying hills several hundred feet away. Still daylight, but dark, it rained hard. The steady, heavy, torrential downpour pounded on the battered roof—the only sound. With no gunfire or excited voices outside, the morning raid had obviously ended.

I tried to rise, but a sharp pain stopped me and my head spun out of control. Drenched in sweat, with mud and blood covering my clothes, I put my hand to my face. My mustache felt wet and matted, and a salty taste filled my mouth.

Shit. I'm bleeding from my nose and mouth. You're in a living hell. They're going to shoot or hang you. Laila, my lovely wife, you won't know what happened.

Uncontrollable panic took over. Silent horror grasped me. I slowly curled up into a ball.

Now the man stood a few feet from me. I could barely make out the outline of his uniform, the PDPA Afghan uniform—a sergeant by rank. My head still spun like a whirling dust devil. A throbbing pain seized the back of my neck.

"Would you like some tea?" the sergeant asked politely.

I couldn't respond. In desperation I tried to speak, but nothing would come out.

The sergeant, fat, and smelling of perspiration, struggled as he picked up my wiry, 160-pound frame from the ground. I screamed out in agonizing pain. With my entire weight upon his, he dragged me over to a chair a few feet away. I slumped down on the seat, ready to collapse.

He put his wide face directly in front of mine. "Would you like some tea?" he asked again, forcing a grin.

I was still in a haze.

"Tea?" he patiently repeated.

"Yes," I finally whispered.

His sly smile and taunting eyes gave me the creeps. The sergeant turned around and waved with his hand, towards a pitch black area to the left of me. He then rushed back to the opening of light and disappeared.

I looked over to my left where the sergeant had signaled, to check out the situation. I barely distinguished two men sitting around a small table. The ends of the their cigarettes glowed. They faced my direction and just stared. Not a sound. A sinister chill overcame me. I closed my eyes.

This is not happening.

Finally, I opened my eyes to see the sergeant coming through the light that now defined the door of an adjoining hallway.

He carried the tea over to the two men in the corner.

They quietly exchanged a few words. Then the sergeant walked over to me and handed me a cup.

"Drink while it's hot," he said, and grinned again.

With both hands, I slowly raised the cup to my shivering lips and took a sip of the steaming tea. It warmed my throat.

I took another soothing sip.

The two men got up from the table and walked over to us, interrupting my small moment of relief. Both Afghan officers—one, a captain, the other, a lieutenant—probably KhAD intelligence agents for the Soviets. Each carried a heavy, military billy club.

The slender lieutenant made the best of his physique— he puffed his chest out like a cocky rooster. His captain, a huge man of over six feet, possessed stern, piercing eyes.

"Take another drink," the lieutenant instructed.

I anxiously put the tea to my mouth and gulped another taste, and as I lowered the cup, the captain hit it out of my hand with his club.

"Our men are searching right now for the satchel you took from the dead man. Did you hide it outside the fort's walls or did you pass the bag along to another man fighting with your group? They will find it in the very near future, especially when the rain lets up, so why don't you just tell us where it is now? We'll let you go if you just tell us."

Looking directly into his eyes I said, "I don't know what you are talking about."

"You bastard!" He struck me in the face with his club, knocking me to the floor.

The three of them rushed me and started to kick me in my ribs and my head. Dazed, I rolled into a tight ball in anguishing pain. My screams were met with smug laughter.

A boot struck me in the face. I saw a flash of white, then everything went black.

CHAPTER 2

The Day Before

A narrow stream of light came through the small window and broke the darkness of my cramped hotel room in downtown Peshawar. I paced the twelve-foot width between the wall, thinking anxiously about the past two years of fighting with the Afghan resistance and analyzing my work with the CIA from this Pakistani hellhole.

The news of the Soviet's sudden military invasion came to me while living in New York with my wife, Laila. Three weeks later I traveled to Karachi to support the cause, and within a week, I had made contact with the right people in the resistance movement. Because of my perfect English, they quickly teamed me up with the CIA as a go-between for the Mujahidin leaders within my group. Soon thereafter, the agency also made me a recruiter of Afghan refugees to help keep watch over the KGB informants who might infiltrate the resistance efforts in Pakistan.

During the past year, I had trooped with the Mujahidin in and out of Southern Afghanistan on raids at least four times. Extremely tired and emotionally beat, I seriously considered leaving the resistance to return to my wife in New York. The Afghanistan I had known in my youth was gone. *Abdul, get out of this damnation and resume your life—start a family, for God's sake!*

I plopped down on my narrow bed, and folded a pillow to rest my aching head. Outside the room's window, large, dense rain clouds loomed. Late March, the heavy monsoon season, had arrived. A major storm fast approached from the Southwest over the Indian Ocean.

Peshawar, located on the Afghan-Pakistani border, served as the perfect city for collaboration between the various Afghan resistance groups and the Central Intelligence

Agency, and provided a convenient spot for the KGB to watch our movements. We had a definite advantage over the Russians since we could blend in with the local Pakistanis.

My thoughts lingered some time among the darkening clouds outside before the abrupt interruption as the front door swung wide open. My best friend, Shah hastily stepped in. He had that wild look in his eyes I had grown to know the past several months.

"Get Up, Abdul. Get Up! We're leaving this afternoon for another raid in Afghanistan, near Kabul, an ammo depot. Get Up. Praise Allah!"

I did not respond.

"What's wrong, my brother, are you not well?"

"I'm not going this time. I need some rest, a long rest, as a matter of fact. I've decided to go back to the United States to my wife."

Shah's eyes became sullen within his hardened broad face. He stroked his short, stubby beard.

"Listen, Shah, I've had it. When I'm not on a mission, I'm the main contact between our people and the CIA. You know I've only worked with them in order to help our country, as a patriot. But, I've had it. I'm always watching my back. It's madness, constantly dodging any possible KGB tails when I deliver and take messages between those American agents and our people."

"Yes, I know what it's done to you. You've been a great asset to the Mujahidin by working with the CIA."

"Fuck, you don't even trust the CIA. Don't patronize me. Damn right I'm tired. I'm sick of this charade, every time I go out, changing my appearance from a local Pakistani to a western business man wearing Foster Grants."

Shah stood silent.

"You know what's sad? I'm getting so good at this spy business, the locals haven't taken notice. Of course, what the hell do they care, they're Pakistanis? They're in a world of their own. They don't have to worry about who's watching them. Always having to look over my shoulder eats away at my nerves. I'm a business manager, not a cloak-and-dagger man."

"I know you are tired. You have fought hard. But the Mujahidin need you on this raid. Fight next to me this time—no medical duty. Just one more for the cause? Together, one more time. Please."

"No, I've done my duty to my country—what's left of it. It's time to go back home. Laila and I want to have children. We need each other. We want to get on with our lives. This place is a nightmare. I don't want to die in this madness."

"Abdul?"

"No."

We stared at each other.

"Do it for your brother—your cousins. Avenge their murders. Don't let their deaths be for nothing."

Silence.

"Abdul, come with us today, for our nation—in the name of Allah. Just one more mission. I beg of you."

I said nothing.

"I'll be back for your final answer in a short while. I'm going down the hall to rouse Zahir and his men. Reconsider, my dear friend."

I stared at the ceiling as he left the room and tried fighting off the gnawing decision I had to make. After a few minutes, my mind drifted back to Christmas, 1978 in New York, when I'd received the horrible phone call from my brother, Assad, in Kabul. The phone call that put me in this hotel room, this forsaken hell.

*   *   *

I had lived in Manhattan for over eight years. I came to America on a special State Department program to attend college. The United States issued grants to only a handful of Afghans to experience what western democracy had to offer. After graduation, I got my first professional job with an off-Broadway theater as their business manager. Then I met an Afghan woman that put a flame in my heart. I was elated. The American dream was becoming a reality.

The call that would change my life came one evening after a successful night at the theater. While tallying the receipts for the night performance of Camelot, the phone in the box office rang. The ticket clerk answered, and after a few moments, turned around to me. From the look on her face, I sensed something terrible had happened.

"Mr. Barkzi, it's one of your brothers on the phone."

"I'll take it upstairs."

By the time I made it upstairs and opened the door to my mezzanine office, my stomach had started to churn. When I picked up the phone, my hand shook.

"Hello?," my voice cracked.

"Abdul! It's me, Assad," he said. "They murdered our brother Mohammed last night—right in front of our house— in front of our family! They just drove right up to the house and took him out and shot him right in the street. They kept shooting him until he didn't move. Abdul, the Afghan communist bastards killed our dear brother!"

I collapsed to my knees. The phone dropped out of my hands to the floor.

"Abdul! Abdul!" The hysterical cries in the background from the whole family could be heard from over the receiver.

I slowly picked up the phone, in a trance, and cradled it

to my ear. The wailing cries of my family spun around and around in my head creating vivid pictures of them in their horrible anguish.

*　　*　　*

"Abdul," a voice called out.

I came out of my trance at the sound of Shah's voice. He had returned to my room and stood in front of the bed—waiting for my final answer. "Are you coming to fight with me, my brother?"

"Yes," I replied. "One last time."

Within the hour I made a quick trip across town to Joe, my immediate field supervisor with the CIA. I had to tell him of the new mission and exchange pertinent information that might be timely for our effort. He and I got along well. He was a pleasant man, with a decent sense of humor.

I took Joe by surprise when I walked through the door of his import/export front. He had found the place on the top floor of the four-story business complex on the outer East side. His Langley boss, Al Taylor, sat across from his desk with several files of paperwork in his lap—obviously they were in the middle of one of Al's impromptu meetings he held with Joe every month.

"Abdul, What a pleasure. Come have a seat," Joe said. As he took his big feet off his desk. He made a pretty funny scene dressed as a Pakistani trader—with a pillbox hat, long loose pajama dress, and thong sandals. He completed his charade having dyed his natural blonde hair black. It complemented a dark, dusty complexion—a result of the pharmaceutical tablets he took on a monthly basis courtesy of the agency. He was in his late thirties.

I laughed. "Feel like you're right at home in your own executive suite, eh Joe?"

He grinned, as he grabbed a chair and placed it next to Al. Al Taylor never smiled, at least not in front of me.

"Hello, Al, haven't seen you for several months. How are things back in the states?"

"Fine, just fine," he replied, lowering his half-frame spectacles over on his long, narrow nose.

Al looked much older than fifty. His hair had turned white from the tours of prior field service, and he needed the cheaters to read all the paperwork he sifted through on a daily basis.

"How are things at your end?" asked Al.

"Not bad," I answered, gritting my teeth, lips tight. *Just one more mission and I'm out of here.*

"So what brings you in now?"

I turned to address both of them. "We're going to take out an ammunitions fort depot tomorrow morning. I leave with my group in less than two hours. I'll be fighting this time."

"Shit, Abdul. Stay behind with the command and medical crew," Joe said, shooting a quick glance over to Al.

"Where?" asked Al.

"Several hours away from Kabul is all I know. Won't know the exact place until we are in the pass. Normal security precautions, you know."

"There's talk, the main electrical plant for Kabul might be a target for destruction. Any connection?" Al blinked.

"Don't know. You know the routine."

"Sure."

Joe cradled his head in his large hands, propping his long, lanky legs up on the desk again. "Hey, Abdul, how's everything going with you and your field agents? Everyone happy?"

"Everyone is content ever since I delivered their cash payments to them last weekend. They appreciated the bonus of five hundred bucks, this time around."

"You and your recruits deserve it. One hell of a month," Joe said, showing his bright all-American smile.

"Damn right they do. Anyway, thanks."

Al lit up a cigarette. He put the gold lighter back into his inside pocket of the tan blazer that topped off his white slacks and shirt. He never dressed as a local. Al always came looking like an American businessman. He didn't give a damn who saw him, though he always took care about the way he entered Joe's office.

"Well, gentlemen, I have another appointment on the other side of town," Al said, as he stood up. "Joe, I ought to be back in a couple of hours and we'll finish our business. Abdul, good to see you in good health. Be careful out there."

"Thanks. Have a good trip back to the States. Just keep sending us money," I said, grinning.

Al's large steel-blue eyes might have flinched a bit, but no other change showed on his deadpan face. He placed the files on the desk, quickly put out his cigarette in the ashtray, and walked straightaway through the back room archway to exit via the back stairs. Al gave a slight wave, never looking back.

"He's never been your cup of tea, has he?" asked Joe.

"Al's all right. It takes all types."

"Yes, that's true. He's pulled me out of some sticky situations the past ten years. Good man, I owe him. But, he's not exactly the type to invite over to a friendly cocktail party in your home."

I smiled.

"I can't believe you're going into the thick of things this

time. Can I ask why?"

"Shah talked me into it. He wants me to be next to him on this mission. He knows how to manipulate, all right."

"He doesn't care much for you working for us, does he?"

"Can't blame him. He's seen the promises that other foreign governments have promised to our leaders in the past, when they really didn't plan to keep them."

"True."

"He likes the American money given to the Mujahidin cause."

"Yes." Joe paused. "Say, have your heard from your wife lately? Any mail?"

"Not for several weeks," I said, looking off for a moment.

"You miss her. I miss Sheila as well. But, I've been doing this for years. She and I are both numb to it, I guess."

Nice.

"Hey, I have a good one for you," Joe said. "Remember those three truckloads of brand-new wool blankets I finally got in from Turkey, for the needy families in the Afghan refugee camps? Well, you won't guess where they turned up—at least part of them last week."

"Where?" I asked with a smirk.

"In the city of Rawalpindi. I had just visited one of my operatives and was walking to my car when a group of young boys came up to me with arms full of spanking brand new blankets identical to the ones we gave away. So I looked at the label on one of the top blankets and sure enough they were one and the same. The boys demanded five American dollars a piece for them. Told me it was a good deal." Joe laughed loudly.

I smiled.

Well, Joe, at least you've kept your sense of humor.

"This war business never ceases to amaze me." Joe smiled.

"No kidding."

"Anything on your mind, Abdul?"

I stared at him for few seconds. "I've just about had it. This might be my last mission with the Mujahidin, and the last of my work with you and the agency."

Joe abruptly took his feet off the desk and sat straight up in his chair. His pleasant smile disappeared. A worried look came over him like he had just found out one of his children were deadly ill.

"You're cooked?"

"All the way through. I can't take the hypocrisy anymore."

Joe stared down at his desk for a moment, picked up his pack of Winstons, flipped a cigarette into his mouth and lit up. He took a long drag and exhaled slowly.

"I don't blame you. When you get back into Peshawar, I'll get the ball rolling to have you out and back home as quickly as possible," he said. "We'll need to debrief for several days, and then you're out of here. Back to your lovely wife, Laila—just like that."

"Are you disappointed?"

"You took me by surprise, that's all." He grinned. "No, Abdul, I don't blame you at all. You've done more than most. I'll miss your excellent work, and your friendship."

"Likewise," I said, softly.

"Cheer up! You'll be enjoying a slice of thin-crusted cheese pizza within a week. I'm jealous."

CHAPTER 3

Towards the Fort

*T*he rains came mid-afternoon.

Two hours later, our troop of eighty-four freedom fighters gathered on the outskirts of Peshawar to head towards the Afghanistan border. Our target, a Russian-Afghan ammo fort, was approximately 100 kilometers Southwest.

Haji, our General Commander, had a wide frame that towered above the troops. His large forehead protected a brilliant mind. A trained military man, Haji once served as an officer in Afghanistan's former royal government forces. He commanded our total respect.

We gathered around him in a large circle, for a briefing of our target. Haji's voice boomed out, "My dear fellow brothers, thank you for again coming to fight for freedom."

Our loud cheers echoed high off the walls of the frozen granite canyon that surrounded us, our weapons raised high in salute. Two alarmed hawks bolted from their nest high above and flew away, sounding screeches into the crisp air.

"Allah smiles upon us for our bravery to save our homeland from the jaws of communist paganism and corruption."

Cheers and weapons raised again in unison.

"Our path leads us to another important mission. There is a fort depot located about ten kilometers away from Kabul's main electrical plant. We are to destroy the munitions, the communications center, and the military equipment within the walls, which includes more than a half-a-dozen tanks. Our successful raid will, at the same time, create a diversion for another major attack by other Mujahidin on the main power plant itself, within minutes after the start of our siege."

Haji raised both of his large, powerful arms into the air. "We will be victorious. Give praise to Allah!"

"Allah Akbar!   Allah Akbar!   Allah Akbar!" everyone proudly chanted on.   We exchanged firm hugs and wished each other safe-keeping for the mission ahead.

Then, we set forth on our way.   As always, we didn't take the main road that snaked through the Kyber Pass.   Beautiful scenery surrounded the ravine we chose to travel. Mountainous ridges rose high into the sky like sentinels of time.   Pockets of red, amber, and green foliage dotted the slopes of the lower hills.

Our passage proved difficult, due to the mud from the rains, and the scattered patches of snow and ice.   However, the steady drizzle of rain did not dampen our ambitious spirit.

The expansive terrain along the pass always served as my savior.   Its magnificence gave me the internal strength to fight.   Having to kill was a painful, yet, in a way, a natural healing experience for what the Afghan communists and Soviets had done to the members of my family—my people.

"I want to kill them ...to kill them!" I yelled at the top of my lungs into the cold air.

Jagged cliffs that towered out of sight into the dark clouds devoured my voice.   No words echoed back.

What a crazy thing to cry out, I thought.   Those majestic mountains were indifferent to my thoughts.   I felt I was just one small pebble amidst these millions of stones.

"Soon you'll have your revenge for their blood lust," a voice shouted back.   It was Shah.

He jogged up to me and gave me a sturdy slap on my back. "Soon, Abdul, soon."

A distant sound like rolling thunder reverberated from the south.

"Probably a few Russian MiG 21s on patrol.   Our men will now keep their eyes peeled towards the sky," Shah said.

The Soviets used the MiGs mainly for direct strikes against our encampments and convoys. What the mountain villagers in this region feared most were the Russian Hind 24 helicopter gunships—the ultimate terror of the Afghan skies. These huge, hovering horrors would sneak up on a village and level it in less than fifteen seconds, with no escape from their ungodly, fiery hell. The Mi 8 choppers—gutted ships used primarily for Russian troop transports—usually followed right behind. They transported hardened paratroopers to man various outposts throughout the northeast Afghan border and handled special raids.

"Shah, nightfall is creeping upon us."

"Yes, we will be hiking all night long. No time to stop for refreshment or sleep this time. We should arrive just before dawn, God willing, in the steep hills that surround the depot. The depot fort itself is located within a cluster of villages in a small valley. Have you been there before?"

"No, I've never been in that area."

"Okay. Once we are in the lower hills, our men will retrieve our main cache of heavy weapons and missile launchers. We hid them away in different spots several weeks ago. How do you feel?"

"I can walk forever."

The Baretta 9mm pistol Joe gave as a gift from the states fit snugly inside my brand new leather coat. Khaki pants and an Afghan pillbox hat pulled tightly over my head completed my uniform. The fully insulated coat was one of several leather coats I had just bought in Peshawar for my wife and myself to take on my hopeful trip back to New York at the time, I thought.

My Laila, soon after this mission, I will wear this on the plane flying home to you, my lovely.

The rest of the men wore the more traditional villager clothing made-up of several layers of long white or beige cotton tops they could place over their bodies for camouflage, when prone on the ground. A wrapped turban covered their heads, though a few donned a pillbox hat like my own. From the air they would blend in with the sand and rock.

Soon, a crescent moon lit our way through the pass. Within the hour, other Mujahidin would meet us. Large, tarp-covered Toyota pickup trucks secured from the local villages would take us further towards our confrontation with the communists. A long night lay ahead.

Finally we came across our fellow brothers. We hugged each other quietly, with a few whispers exchanged between family and friends. All of us quickly jumped into the back of the trucks and took off. Our eyes glowed like fireflies. Even the moon smiled upon us, though only a slight smile.

The rough, high-desert road to the next mountain pass was mired in mud. The trucks rode low to the ground from the overload of our troops. I felt every grind of the gears below me. All of the trucks were long overdue for repairs.

Our destiny again awaited before us. But, somehow I had a lot of apprehension about what lay ahead for me.

During our arduous caravan to the next pass, I struck up a conversation with Farouk, a local sheep herder from a small village on the outskirts of the city, Ghanzi. He told me how he had lost his three children along with his only two sisters to a Russian sneak attack that occurred while he and his wife went away for staples and supplies. His eyes burned with animosity. His voice quaked as he spoke in monotone—barely audible over the pickup truck's laboring engine.

"It happened the last week of August. We had been gone only a day, when the Soviets came. Kashmir, my wife's grandfather was severely wounded in the initial attack. The old man watched the ensuing torture while lying speechless on the ground and later told me of the horror, which I shall now tell you.

"It was late morning. The women and elders in the village were taking a break from the morning's work. The men were out for the day, tending the sheep in the next canyon.

"The children ran around, in and out of the houses, laughing and playing. Everyone else had lain down to rest from the rising heat and gusty winds. Then, all of a sudden, the children froze, and looked straight up into the sky. Their cheerful laughter turned into dreadful, dead silence.

"The village knew the sound—the horrible sound of the unholy Soviet gunships. They came from behind the mountainous ridge that for generations had enclosed and protected our village from the harsh winters. The ridge that had once been our protector had become their shield.

"Before the women could find their children, the bullets and explosions of missiles engulfed the village. This was immediately followed by two or three napalm missiles. The village became an inferno from hell. The explosions' deafening roar silenced all the screams from our people. It was over in a minute."

Farouk hesitated, his pain apparent. The men in the back now listened also, their heads low.

"The Russian paratroopers were upon them, kicking and shoving our wounded and bewildered around. They were shouting, 'Where is your Allah now, you scum? Where is your Allah now?'

"They gathered all the women, children, and the two elders still standing, and forced them into a straight line. A KhAD Afghan officer, along with the paratroopers, pulled the two elders out of line, and asked them where the younger men were. The old men told them that they were out in the next gully, herding sheep. The Russian soldiers called them filthy liars, pushed them to the ground, and shot them.

"Then they pulled three pregnant women out of the line and asked them where their husbands were. The women cried, as they told them the same thing. The soldiers called their husbands murderous Mujahidin and screamed that the babies they carried would be murderers too. Then they took their rifles with bayonets and disemboweled them in front of everyone, yelling, 'Your children will not live to kill us. Die, bastards. Die, you scum!'

"The screams were ungodly. The women huddled on the ground over their gasping fetuses in their arms. They died in slow, ugly agony. The soldiers then pushed the rest of the remaining women and children into a hut. Without hesitation, they barred the door and threw several grenades in through the windows to finish the job."

Farouk's voice cracked. "On the way out, they poisoned the wells. Kashmir said the bastard soldiers laughed all the way back to their damn helicopters.

"This is why I've joined the Jihad, the Mujahidin. Forgive me Allah, but I want due revenge!" Farouk slowly dropped his face and cupped his shaking hands over his face, crying quietly.

Everyone fell silent for the remainder of the ride to our destination. An out-of-control fire burned in my gut in hatred of the communists' bloody hands.

At last, we arrived to hike our final mountain passage to the fort. Within four hours it would be daylight. We said our farewells to our compatriots and started afoot for our final ascent between two, small, snowcapped peaks. Every footstep reminded us of our date with the enemy. We arrived, several long hours later, in the lower hills and gathered the weapons from our hidden caches.

During the hour or so before the siege, we rested. Commander Haji then led us in our morning prayer. After group prayer, Shah and I put our hands on each others' shoulders and said the victory prayer together—preparing ourselves spiritually and mentally for the fight ahead.

"Right after this mission, Abdul, you will be back on your way to Laila in New York. You'll be happy having put another thorn into the Russians' souls. They deserve everything they get for brainwashing our youth, then invading our homes and butchering our families."

"I know, I know, God willing." I hesitated. "Shah, you know that in the past I've usually remained in the back with the commanders providing covert intelligence information, and then, after the shooting stopped, helped the doctor with what limited medical assistance I could offer. But now, I will attack with you—killing on the front line. Allah, give me the strength."

"He will." Shah smiled. "In the event we don't take out the compound this morning, Commander Haji has plans for a second attempt at sundown. We will prevail."

The entire troop headed for their positions. The hearty crows of the roosters in the surrounding villages proudly announced the morning. The pride in our hearts matched the cocks' vigilance.

We divided up into three groups. One group, the main thrust, would attack straight into the front of the fort. The other two planned to split apart to handle both the left and right flanks of the assault. Shah would lead my assigned group to attack the left side of the fortress. I carried an AK-47 supplied to us from the CIA—spoils from the Vietnam War in fairly decent condition, considering its age.

Commander Haji would signal the missile launchers to start the attack with about ten minutes of bombardment before our men advanced for the siege. Our group set up for the descent about one meter away, directly under the launchers for the west side of the depot.

Through the faint amber light of the rising sun, I could make out the outline of the majestic fort, which sat atop a sloping, rocky hill, overlooking the valley. It was the first time I had laid eyes on it.

Shah whispered, "She's beautiful, yes? It was built during the British Anglo-Afghan Wars in 1839. A testimony to the great military architecture of the fourth Century B.C., when Alexander the Great conquered Afghanistan. It reminds you of the famous Citadel built by Alexander's forces in Herat, only on a smaller scale, yes?"

I nodded.

"The walls are over fifteen feet high, with the ramparts and enclosed sentry towers of that era. Really magnificent, don't you agree?"

"Yes," I quietly replied. "Now we have to assault this historic monument violated by those communist bastards. We'll make them pay for everything they have done."

Shah bowed his head solemnly in agreement.

The sentry towers—one on all four corners, and two right over the main gate—held two armed Afghan soldiers. Each pair manned a mounted heavy machine gun, at least fifty-caliber or better. Our rocket launchers, set up in the mountains rising above the fortress, would hopefully destroy the two towers up front and on both sides of the front wall.

All along the front, Afghan troops stood watch. Below, razor-wire fences lined the ancient ramparts, most likely mined, with controllable remote detonators in the towers.

The remaining towers at the rear of the compound would fall from the fire power of our tripod fifty-caliber machine guns. Our two flanks had positioned them up at the far east and west perimeter local. Two smaller, wooden-gate entrances, located at the west and east sides of the fort walls, served as our planned, two points of forced entry.

We held, in reserve, one Stinger missile, the only one we could get, to blast the Soviet jet or helicopter backup that would probably arrive from Kabul before the fighting ended. The bastards always did.

The mission's two main objectives stood inside the compound. The munitions building and the communications center were located right behind the main command center. Haji gave us an updated report pinpointing about one hundred and twenty-five soldiers and a good dozen PDPA officers. The scouts counted ten Soviet tanks parked along the back wall of the fort—icing on the cake.

Shah and I positioned ourselves behind a huge boulder, seventy meters from the left side of the fort. Everyone else in our group had fanned out a good twenty feet apart behind shoulder-height boulders.

Suddenly a loud swish of air passed directly over my head, followed immediately by a deafening explosion at the wall directly in front of me. Pieces of the fort's wall and dust showered our position. Seconds later, more rockets pounded into the ramparts and walls, bringing the morning tranquillity to an abrupt end. After about fifteen minutes of shelling, our group started to work slowly towards the west side of the compound, firing our machine guns. The serene valley had turned into an insane hell.

The left front tower was out of commission. But along the west wall, a dozen soldiers fired their machine guns and grenade launchers towards our position. The deafening roar of the guns and the missile explosions swelled my eardrums with a horrendous, high-pitched ring.

After five or six clips, I looked over to Shah. His eyes bulged with the intensity of the fight. They protruded out from his drawn, sun-blackened face covered with a dripping-wet beard. His stocky frame held the gun with a tight vengeance, as the barrel's tip turned ashen white.

My eyes darted back and forth. I could see that we had heavy casualties. A Soviet rocket had dismembered two men, previously stationed together, just twenty yards to my left.

God, they never knew what happened. Allah, take them.

Our cover, at best minimal, served our needs. No one ran. We wanted them.

"We'll rid the fort of these infidels!" I shouted.

The distant sound of Soviet MiGs could be heard coming from the direction of the capitol. We kept steadfast to our mission.

I'll kill you Russian imperialists and Afghan traitors. You shot my brother and cousins. I will get you.

The firefight raged, as the MiG 21 jet fighters entered the valley. They didn't even come close to the fort, as they strafed missiles over the villages that surrounded the area.

"Come get us... not the women and children, you cowards. Come get us," I screamed.

After several minutes, and what seemed like an eternity, the jet fighters left, leaving the valley in flames.

Then we heard another trembling sound. The Soviet Hind 24 helicopters came right over the mountaintop behind us. Shah waved us off the attack. Our men ran back to safety into the mountainside. The gunship's missiles exploded within a hundred yards from our position, causing me to lose my balance for several moments.

I turned around for one last look at the fortress, as I rose from the safety of the boulder. An Afghan man in civilian clothing ran out from the fort's side gate.

I figured he must be an Afghan who was perhaps, forced to fight against us, and now escaping his plight to join the Mujahidin.

I'll wait for him.

He ran like the devil loomed behind him. I frantically waved at him to come on. While he ran, not more than a hundred feet away, a gunship missile landed right behind him, and propelled him in the air. He dropped right in front of me. I looked over at him.

He was dead.

I bent over to close his eyes. About my age, I thought... twenty-two.

As I stepped back, I noticed a leather satchel around his neck. I hesitated.

What the Hell!

I pulled the strap over his head and looked inside the bag.

Shit, he's a jewel carrier! There are handfuls of precious stones here—rubies, emeralds, and sapphires!

A bullet brazed my ear.

Panicked, I ran to the back side of the boulder and swiftly dug a hole in the mud with my hands as fast as I could. I dropped the satchel into the shallow hole and quickly covered it up.

More bullets whizzed right over my head.

I grabbed my AK-47 and ran like hell, towards the protection of the mountain. A Russian gunship lurked right behind me. As I ran a few more yards ahead, a thunderous explosion filled the sky, illuminating the dark morning like a bright noon sun. I looked behind me to see the gunship engulfed in a huge fire ball, dropping like a rock to the ground, fifty yards behind.

They took it out with our Stinger missile. Yes!

I took off again, as fast as my feet could move, to rejoin my fellow Mujahidin. More gunships came right over me—adrenaline raced through my mind and body.

Damn it!

I then faintly remember an another explosion.

The moment froze in time—no missiles, no yells, no screams—just the bright fire of the jewels.

And, that's when I came to and realized my predicament—a prisoner beaten unconscious, in the fort compound, lying prostrate on an army cot in the same room where the KhAD had interrogated me earlier.

Now an Afghan man leaned over me, as he carefully cleaned off the dried blood on my face.

He looks like a nice man, with a compassionate heart. Hopefully not like the bastards who beat me.

"The percussion of the missile that exploded behind you caused a lot of bleeding from your nose and ears. Those blows and kicks the KhAD officers gave you didn't help. I'm going to bandage and wrap your ribs. Don't worry, I'm a doctor. Try to relax." He paused, then whispered, "I'm sorry about what happened to you."

I said nothing. I stared at the ceiling.

He cleaned my lacerations, bandaged me up, and gave me a shot. "This will help ease your pain and also help you sleep. Good luck to you." The doctor gave me a warm smile

and left the room through the brightly lit door. I could barely see him as he stood next to a man, whom I couldn't make
out. They conversed briefly, then disappeared.

I lay there for several minutes trying to clear my foggy
mind in order to consider my predicament. But the medica-
tion, along with the continuous, mesmerizing sound of the
rain outside the fort's window, started to take its effect. I
drifted off to sleep.

When I awoke I raised my bandaged head to look
around. It felt like it had been hit by a sledgehammer.

*Hell, I'm still here. This isn't just a bad nightmare. Dear
God, help me.*

I looked out the window. The rain had not subsided. It
seemed very late in the day. My cot was right next to the
chair I sat in when they had started to interrogate me earlier.
The KhAD officers had vacated the table in the dark area
along the wall.

I turned to check out the lit door again. A Russian
Colonel came into view. He smiled broadly as he walked up
to me.

To have a high-ranking officer here in this remote outpost
was completely baffling. The leaders always stayed in Kabul.

Why has he shown himself?

"Hello, my friend. How are you doing? Better?" He
spoke in perfect Farci.

Still stunned by his presence, I said nothing.

"My apologies, for the officers beating you like that.
They are overzealous towards the communist cause. I'm
truly sorry for their behavior. My own Russian comrades,
mostly Bolsheviks, do not behave that way. We are more civ-
ilized, you see. Would you like some tea?" he asked.

I hesitantly nodded yes, remembering my earlier ordeal.

"I'm Colonel Kirsch of the Soviet Army. And what might be your name?"

"Abdul."

"Abdul, a very humble name. It means servant of God, does it not?"

I looked into his blue-gray eyes, tried to read the man's true intentions, and nodded my head, yes.

"Well, Abdul, you look quite a bit different than most Mujahidin I have come across—shorter hair; clean shaven, except for your trimmed mustache. Have you traveled to the West, perhaps?

"No."

"I see. Well, let's say that you have at least acquired some Western tastes judging from the sidearm we found on you containing American serial numbers. No?"

He turned around and walked in deliberate, long strides towards the door—tall, slender, about fifty years old... yet in great shape. Most probably a descendant of a long line of arrogant Bolshevik military officers.

Going to save the world are you? Bastard!

The colonel returned with two cups of tea. He handed one to me, and then took a sip of his own. He pulled up another chair and sat down right in front of me.

I put the hot cup of tea to my lips and instantly jerked back in pain. The KhAD captain's blow with his club had left a badly cut lip.

Colonel Kirsch frowned at my swollen mouth. "Again, my sincere apologies for the KHAD's cruel behavior towards you. Let the tea cool a bit, and then you can sip it."

I mustered a slight smile. My face hurt like hell.

"Well, Abdul. The captain tells me you might have something belonging to us. Do you remember taking a leather satchel from a civilian who ran from our outpost? One of our men, stationed on the wall, saw you take the bag. Remember?"

Silence.

"I realize you're probably still somewhat in shock from your dramatic experience. Try to think, now. Is your memory coming back to you?"

I stared down at my cup.

"Abdul, the contents of the satchel belongs to us. Please tell us what you did with it. Did you or did you not pass it off to one of your fellow Mujahidin as you retreated? We have searched everywhere, since your men retreated this morning. We know that you, personally, took the bag. It wasn't on you when we found you."

I said nothing.

"Please try to cooperate with us. You will make it a lot easier on yourself. Tell us where it is and we will let you go—with no more questions. You will be free to leave, when we find it. Trust me, Abdul."

I barely got the words out. "There was a lot of smoke and dust from the guns and missile explosions," I stuttered. "They must have mistaken me for someone else. I don't have any idea what you are talking about."

His face turned red. "Abdul, do you take me for a fool? Our men said it was you. You were the only one wearing a leather jacket, and a new one at that!"

Shit.

"I have been very reasonable with you. Don't make this any worse on yourself than it has to be. Tell me, and you can go free. Tell me!"

"I don't know where any bag is. You have the wrong man."

You're going to have me killed anyway, even if I tell you where the jewels are.

"You fool. You will give us the location of that satchel, damn you!"

The colonel abruptly rose from his chair and without hesitation, walked quickly, in his arrogant, long steps back through the door behind him.

What is next, Allah? Give me courage.

I felt as if I had lived through an eternity, since he had charged through the door. The bright light now came across as the flames of hell.

Outside the window, the darker sky meant dusk was coming.

If they started to torture me, I would hold on—just hang in there a little bit longer. Commander Haji planned a second attack at sundown. It could happen any time now.

Suddenly, two familiar figures appeared. My body tightened with intense fear. The two damned KhAD officers arrogantly headed towards me. I tried to swallow, but couldn't.

"Well, well, Abdul. Colonel Kirsch told us he couldn't reason with you," the captain blurted out.

"He questions your honesty and feels that you chose not to give back what belongs to us. What a shame. Well, my stupid friend, he has asked us to be a little more direct with you."

The captain backhanded me in the face. "I think he has made a wise decision, don't you agree?"

They both laughed. Their ice cold smiles sent a quick shiver down my body. My head started to spin.

"Abdul, one last time. What happened to the bag?"

"Fuck you, bastards. I don't have it!"

The big lieutenant hit me solidly and squarely on the jaw.

I couldn't feel my face. Warm blood flooded my mouth and flowed down my throat. I started to gag uncontrollably. I put my hands to my face.

He broke my jaw!

"Bastards, you say? Listen here, you bastard. Tell us where the bag is, or we'll cut your nuts off. You stupid fucking bastard!"

I rasped as I tried to yell back, but couldn't.

The lieutenant shoved me off the chair. Both men kicked me in the ribs again—relentlessly. The sound of cracking ribs from both sides magnified, and I spewed bright red blood.

"Is your God coming to rescue you now?" they asked repeatedly. Their hysterical laughter tormented my mind.

They kicked all over my body until complete numbness replaced the pain.

Laila, I'm going to die...I love you—. I blacked out.

This time, I awoke to find myself hoisted up by my arms from the ceiling in the center of the room. The fat sergeant stood below me. His grin reminded me of a swine.

"We've got a surprise for you Abdul. I'm sure it will come as a real shock to you." He laughed right into my face. His breath reeked of soured goat cheese and cheap wine.

Pig!

He stepped aside to reveal a black box on a cart, which held two cable wires and a wet sponge on each end.

They're going to slowly electrocute me! I don't have much time. Save me Shah! Attack my brothers. Attack this hellhole fortress!

"You will tell us where the satchel is, and then—." The sergeant put his mouth to my ear and whispered, "You will beg us to put a bullet into your putrid head."

Then he abruptly turned around and shouted back towards the door, "We're ready, captain."

The two KhAD officers reappeared and walked slowly

towards me as they smoked their cigarettes like fiends. Their evil smirks made me shudder.

Just as the captain started to say something, a missile exploded right outside the second-story window, followed by several other missiles ramming into the back of the compound. My whole head rang out in pain.

"Cut him down, leave him on the floor and get rid of the box," the captain shouted, as he and the lieutenant quickly turned around and ran back into the next room.

As the sergeant started to cut my leather bindings, his hate-filled eyes glared at me and he snarled, "I'll be back with the box to finish you later."

He cut me loose and I fell to the floor. Then he grabbed the cart and made a quick exit from the room.

The entire command center turned into chaos, filling with anxious shouts and hysterical cries. Deafening explosions rocked the building.

Hardly able to move, I slowly crawled forward to the small table alongside of the wall, for protection. I yelled silently, in excruciating pain, as I struggled to put one arm in front of the other. I finally made it underneath the table and curled up in the fetal position, with my arms covering my head.

Allah! Don't leave me like this. Let my people be victorious. Shah... Shah, please get me out of here!

I cried and prayed for help in my new living hell. Finally the shelling, gunfire, and yelling stopped.

My God, did my people take the fort?

I waited in frozen fear for several long minutes.

Finally a voice shouted out. "Abdul! Abdul! Where are you, my dear brother?"

It's Shah! Yes, it's Shah! They did it!

I started to cry in relief, and joy.

Shah ran into the room, glanced around, saw me, and shouted triumphantly, "Abdul, you're alive!"

He knelt beside me. His eyes filled with tears as he cradled my head in his hands. I gave him a big grin and passed out.

*   *   *

The next day, the sway of the stretcher awakened me from my deep sleep. Focusing through my swollen eyes, I faced Shah, who manned the back of the stretcher. He smiled when he saw me squinting at him.

The rains had stopped, and the early morning sun shone brightly. Its rays felt warm against my face. My Mujahidin compatriots journeyed through the first mountainous pass on the way back to Pakistan border.

Shah's calm voice comforted me. "Good morning, my dear friend. I hope you're feeling better. Please don't try to talk. We had to apply many extra bandages—especially to your broken jaw and ribs. Try to be quiet, and lay still to ease your pain. Here, take this medicine. Put it under your tongue and suck on it slowly."

Zaki, just eighteen years old, came up beside me and put a small wad of a brown, gooey substance into my mouth. Although I had never taken it before, I knew it was opium, having treated our wounded during past missions. I moved it under my tongue and gave him a wink of appreciation, about to experience my first use of an opiate. I hoped for an alleviation of pain and soreness throughout my entire body and closed my eyes to relax.

I fell back fast asleep for at least an hour and reopened my eyes to a dream-like world. I felt no pain, as if my whole body floated on a lofty, surrealistic cloud. The pass had never seemed so vivid to me—the colors and textures of the ground, and the long crevices in the side of the mountain—all so finite. Even the pastel colors of the men's robes seemed to jump out at me. In those moments I forgot about everything that had happened the day before.

Man, this is so beautiful, so fantastic!

I began to giggle. The men took notice and laughed heartily at my opium-induced giddiness. I started to laugh with them, finally breaking out into hysterical laughter. Shah grabbed my hand and softly said to me, "Abdul, I know you're feeling great right now, but try to be still and don't laugh. It's bad for your jaw and rib cage. Try to just smile."

I gave him a smirk that probably appeared childish.

When we finally got back to our base late in the day, Commander Haji made arrangements for my transfer to the main hospital in the city of Peshawar. I left early the next morning after I said all my good-byes to my group. Shah rode in the medical van with me, because he had urgent matters to attend to for the resistance in the city.

During the ride I jotted down a note telling him that I found something special during the firefight at the fort—a godsend—and had hidden it away in a safe place. When he read it, he gave me a quizzical look. I smiled, grabbed another piece of paper and wrote, "I'll tell you about it when I'm out of the hospital. It can wait."

He nodded O.K. "You should just rest and get better. You are lucky to be alive, considering your severe injuries. I'm sure it can wait, like you say." He gave me that great smile of his.

CHAPTER 4

The Weeks After

*M*y long and painful stay in the hospital lasted close to a month. As I went through various stages of surgeries to put me back in one piece, the staff tried to make me as comfortable as possible.

I had been in great shape and energetic since my teenage years, so found the lengthy bed-ridden ordeal a bitch to handle. Shah visited me almost every day which helped keep my spirits up. His cheerful encouragement and constant jokes took away some of the helpless frustration and anger a long hospital stay can breed. Of course, thoughts of the precious jewels lingered in the back of my mind.

On a quiet evening, during one of his visits several days before my release, Shah switched our talk to a more serious tone.

"Abdul. There is talk going around certain circles in Peshawar. The word is, a group of powerful people in Peshawar who run one of the largest smuggling rings of illicit drugs and precious stones have been asking about you. In fact they have already rudely visited a few hotel rooms of several of our fellow Brothers making inquiries. They say you might know the whereabouts of a shipment of expensive jewels that should have been delivered to them here in Pakistan around the time of our raid. Talk is they're dead serious about recovering these stones. Why would they say you might know something about this? This wouldn't have anything to do with the special godsend you came across during the raid, would it?"

I just shrugged my shoulders and grinned.

"Maybe they are mistaken? Yes, brother?"

"Shah, my dear good friend, it's getting late and I'm very tired from a long day of physical therapy. I need to get a good night's rest. Do you mind if I close my eyes?"

His intense, inquisitive stare at me relaxed. "Of course, please forgive me. You do need your rest. I'll stop by tomorrow. The nurse says you'll be getting out in a few days. We'll get together after your release and chat more about such crazy matters as precious gems and the like when you're more up to it." Shah smiled.

"Goodnight, Shah."

"Goodnight, and may Allah bless you, My Dear Friend."

As Shah left, my mind kicked in gear. He knew I'd given him a polite brush-off with my excuse of tiredness. I didn't want to tell him the details of what I had planned for the jewels, until I left the hospital.

The jewels I had almost lost my life for, belonged to those ruthless thugs. The bastards sold us freedom fighters out for profit to whomever they pleased—the Afghan army, Soviet forces, Pakistan, or the KGB. It had turned into a get-rich free-for-all. Even some of our Afghan tribal leaders cashed in on the booty of this bloody war, stashing away huge profits from sales of precious stones and opium into their own pockets. It changed the complexity of the Holy War the Muslims came to fight for.

Those thugs want their precious stones? They can burn in rotten hell. It's my turn to profit now.

The majority of the money came from the illicit drug trade in Afghanistan. Every one of the major seven tribes involved in the Mujahidin had a piece of the opium trade action to help finance their own resistance efforts. The money, supplies, and equipment the United States provided through the Pakistan government didn't come close to effectively supporting the war effort.

Opium grew abundantly in the Eastern plateaus of our

country. Several of the larger tribes actually grew the majority of the poppies harvested for raw opium, then sold it to Afghan drug smugglers who would transport the crude opium in jars on mules and camels, through the Southern Afghan states to the Iran border. As these caravans passed through various tribal lands, they would have to pay each tribe protection money for safe travel through their territory. At the border, the smugglers sold the opium to the Iranian Mafia. From there, the opium was smuggled through Southern Iran and, once at the Turkish border, sold to the Turks who, in turn, processed the opium into raw heroin in their elaborate kitchens, finally ready for selling to the various crime syndicates throughout the world. A well-established, well-oiled drug trade network.

The cream of the money made from raw opium sales and protection fees initially went to the resistance effort, at the beginning of the war. But, in-fighting between the various tribes over territorial lands, and ugly greed, had taken its toll as the war went on, resulting in entrepreneurial dipping into the coffers for personal Swiss bank accounts.

The night after my release from the hospital, Shah joined me for dinner at the hotel where I stayed. I had registered at the quiet, modest, yet comfortable Green Hotel, in downtown Peshawar.

In front of my hotel, on the busy Saddar Road, they had built the brand new Green Hotel. The modern building had become a favorite for a handful of the foreign press who camped out there, however incorrigibles frequented the place also: drug dealers and other fortune seekers taking advantage of the war—an infamous lot of bedfellows. Further down the avenue, about a quarter mile West, the Dean Hotel, housed the majority of the foreign press, important businessmen, and intelligence agents from all over the world. Though I spent a good amount of time meeting people there at the Dean's, I felt content with my lodging at the quaint Green Hotel—a good ways from the zoo down the road.

During our meal in the hotel restaurant, Shah abruptly popped the question to me about the missing jewels. "Abdul, the gangsters' patience is wearing thin, in regards to the lost shipment of jewels. Hell, they came to my house last night. I didn't answer the door. My family hid and cried! Now, are you ready to tell me about what you found during the fight?"

"I wondered when you would ask again," I said. "Do you realize you have been so anxious this evening that you've hardly touched your meal. Eat, the food is very good. The lamb chops are tender. Don't you agree?"

Shah laughed lightly. I noticed a lot of apprehension in his curt smile.

"What did you find that morning?"

"The jewels those animals are looking for, what else? Why do you think I'm still around this hellhole, and not back with my wife in New York?"

"I knew it. How did you come by them?"

I took a long sip of my drink. "Remember when you signaled our group to retreat back into the hillside?"

"Yes."

"Well, as I was firing off a few rounds to fall back, I saw a man running out from the side gate of the fort towards me. I figured he was an Afghan who tired of fighting for the communists, and wanted to join us. So I waited for him and gave him as much cover as possible. Just before he got to me, a gunship missile blew him sky high and landed him right in front of me—right in front of me, Shah. A goner.

"As I further looked him over, I noticed he had a leather

satchel around his neck. I quickly took it off him and looked inside. And, Shah, there lay a large handful of top-quality jewels. Could be worth several million dollars!"

"Oh my God!" Shah's eyes opened wide.

"Anyway, with my bare hands, I quickly buried them right near the boulder I had used as a shield, in the fighting. Nobody but I can find them. I've got a plan. I know how we can retrieve the jewels and sell them for a considerable amount of money—lots of money. Money enough for you and everyone I plan to involve."

"Are you nuts?" Shah said. "They are going to kill you if you don't give the jewels back. You're a madman."

"Shhhh. Someone may hear you."

"You're crazy," he whispered.

"It's O.K., it's O.K. I have a good plan. It will work. Trust me, it will really work."

"I will not hear any of it. They will kill you. And they'll kill me and anyone else who gets involved. You don't know these monsters. They enjoy killing. They thrive on it."

Shah held his breath while I kept my smile.

"Besides, how in the hell do you think we can safely get back to the fort? And, even if we could, we then would have to find the jewels—if they are still there. The heavy rains might have exposed them by now. Perhaps someone at the fort or one of the local villagers has found them already." He paused. "Okay, suppose we do find them—we'd have to get our butts safely out of there and find a country we can escape to, immediately. If we did finally make it, we would have to find a trustworthy connection abroad to buy the jewels." As Shah talked on breathlessly—his eyes bulged.

"We know nothing of this type of business," he continued. "You suggest this far-fetched escapade with these well-connected, bloodthirsty criminals breathing down our necks. Are you insane?"

"Settle down, My Dear Brother. Settle down," I said.

He poured a glass of water and gulped most of it down, without hesitation.

Shah slowly bent over the table, shook his fork at me, and looked straight into my eyes. "It's true, during the fortress raid, the one missile exploded behind the jewel carrier and killed him straight out, but the one that exploded behind you has seemed to have made you a casualty, as well. You may still be alive but, you are not all there in the head. You are not sane. Seriously, only a maniac would expect to outwit and outgun dangerous gangsters."

Shah's serious tone and taut face struck me funny. I broke out in uncontrollable laughter and even spilled my iced tea all over the table linen. Shah's face went bright red. He bolted up from the table and started for the door.

I jumped up, and put both of my arms around him to stop him, still in laughter.

"Shah, please. Come back to the table. Don't be so skeptical. I'm not crazy. In the hospital, I figured everything out. And, it will work. Please come back. Remember, it was you who talked me into going on this last raid, almost costing me my life. You owe it to me to at least hear me out."

He turned around. "All right. I'll listen to your crazy plan, you madman. But, I promise nothing. I'll just listen, do you understand?"

I gave him a big smile. "Of course, dear brother. Come sit back down and enjoy your meal."

Shah barely picked at his food while I started to lay out the details of my plan. But, as I pointed out the particular merits of my approach, which involved several friends we had known since childhood—one his cousin—he relaxed. The lamb chops soon disappeared from his plate. By the end of our talk, he had picked up and savored the bones. We rose from the table and Shah embraced me.

"Let's do it," he said.

The plan involved people Shah and I could rely on—trust with our lives. I needed to get us all together.

*   *   *

The next week, I met several times with Joe at his import office for my final debriefing. During my stay in the hospital, he had taken the initiative to have a private courier give me several verbal messages in regards to other agents sorrow and concern, for my capture and torture. Other than concluding pertinent agency business, he didn't bring up the subject of any rumors on the streets in the way of possible missing jewels. Whether he knew about them and my actual involvement, I couldn't tell—he probably did.

When I left out the front door for the last time, we shook hands firmly. "Good luck! Be careful," Joe said, with a broad smile.

The day after my resignation, I moved out of the hotel and into my cousin's small home, conveniently located behind his photography studio in a small mall off the main thoroughfare in Peshawar. Sher Mohammed's storefront studio provided a perfect place to hold private meetings. I had used his place before, for Mujahidin meetings.

People who wanted to see me regarding sensitive matters casually walked into the front of the studio, and Mohammed's young son then ran out through the rear door to fetch me at the house. I slipped in through the back and rendezvoused inside the darkroom. It provided an excellent setup for the jewel effort.

Sher, ten years my senior, had grown a long graying beard almost down to his waist. Off and on, he had helped with the Mujahidin over the past several years, with Shah and me.

Alone in his studio, a day after I moved into his home, he inquired as to my situation.

"Abdul, what's going on? You're receiving a lot of calls since yesterday, and not the normal Mujahidin contacts. A correct assumption on my part?"

"I had planned to tell you about it. Let's have some tea in the back."

I could trust Sher, though he probably would not take part in the operation. I deeply respected his confidence.

As I told him the whole story of the attack, the jewels, and the plan to recover them to sell, he surprised me by calmly nodding his head in agreement.

"That's more encouragement than I first received from Shah," I said.

"It sounds like you've got the right people for your team. Especially Yosif and Shah's cousin, Farid. They are both in the area right now."

"How is our huge friend, Yosif?" I asked.

"He's doing great. He asked about you when I bumped into him at the Deans Hotel several months ago. As strong as ever. The last I heard, he hadn't married, but is doing well in the business of buying and selling precious jewels. He's still known for that short temper of his. Most competitors instinctively stay out of his way." Sher chuckled.

Yosif, a former body builder and, when in his late teens, a small-time loan shark, remained a good friend to both Shah and me, since childhood.

"What's doing with Farid, lately?" I asked.

"Shah's cousin? He's doing fine too. He's not the physical phenomenon like Yosif, but he's just as cunning."

"Good. How's his enterprising operation of smuggling wealthy businessmen and Islamic professors out of Afghanistan?"

"Still going strong, as far as I know."

Sher correctly assessed Farid's talent. In addition, he was an extremely bright, young man, only in his twenties, well-educated and rich. He came from a wealthy Pashtun family who had established a successful trading business of smuggling durable goods into Afghanistan—desirable goods such as electrical appliances, cotton, and silk that an Afghan family normally would find too costly because of prohibitive import taxes. Since the Soviet takeover, Farid had started his own smuggling ring. He developed a real knack of smuggling Afghans safely into Pakistan and then acquiring the proper forged passports and airline tickets needed to get his clients safely overseas to live.

Quite a few of the families of communist regime officers, who knew the tables could turn in the future, made up Farid's clientele. These officials wanted to ensure their loved ones safety out of the country. This provided Farid with extra protection from the military police when his men met the families on the outskirts of Kabul to begin their trek towards the Pakistan border. Quite a paradox—families of opposing political and moral convictions traveling together to escape the horror of war.

Shah and I agreed upon a bright, attractive, American woman named Stella, a good friend of Yosif's, as the last key person of the team. We had known her back in Kabul in our teens, when she worked for the Peace Corps. She spoke perfect Farci and had gained the respect of most of the men in Kabul's social circles. Sher had met her several times back then.

"Seen Yosif's friend, Stella, lately?" I asked.

"No, but I understand she has been working with Yosif on several business deals—securing airline tickets for his travel here in the East and in Europe. They say she is evasive about her business dealings. Some of the local circles speculate she might also be 'eyes' for the CIA."

No one ever pushed the matter regarding her possible involvement with the CIA. I had never run across her with my dealings with the agency, but that didn't mean anything in the spy business. Whatever she might possibly had done with the agency or to whomever, was her business. All of us trusted her.

*   *   *

Two weeks after my decisive dinner discussion with Shah, we had a meeting for all the principal participants involved—except Stella, leaving it to Yosif to determine her part in the mission.

The group met during the late afternoon. The entire day before, I paced around in Sher's small house, my mouth dry in anticipation of what Yosif and Farid would have to say about my plan. Finally, Sher's son came to fetch me for the meeting. They had all gathered in the darkroom. The bright fluorescence lit the large room, showing the clean, metal developing trays.

"Yosif, Shah, Farid. Thank you for coming!"

Yosif came forward and wrapped his large arms around me. He stood at least 6 ft. 2 in., and his 240 lb. muscular frame looked extremely large for an Afghan. Yosif sported a bold mustache that framed his large protruding jaw and mouth.

His eyes filled with sorrowful tears; he knew of my torture.

"Yosif, it's really good to see you. You're just as I remembered, bigger than life."

Yosif wiped his tears away, and replaced his sadness with a wide smile.

"Likewise." Yosif briskly scrubbed my head with his knuckles and laughed. His hearty voice soothed my ears. "I have confided in Stella. She's in. We need ticket connections, and she knows the right people for this job. I can't wait for you and Shah to see her again."

"Abdul, how are you my dear friend?" said Yosif. "You have really grown. How old are you now, twenty-one?"

"Twenty-three next month! And you? You're now, what, almost thirty years old?"

"Yes, something like that. Time has flown. Remember when I used to bail you and Shah out of trouble from the local gangs who always wanted to kick your butts?"

"Of course. You always saved us. You were our big brother."

"Well, it looks like history is repeating itself again. No?"

We all laughed.

Shah said, "Abdul...Yosif, I want you to meet my cousin, Farid."

"Hello, my dear brothers!" Farid announced. "I've been waiting anxiously to meet all of you."

A robust young man, with a wide, almost chubby face came forward and gave me a hug, and then turned to Yosif who stepped up and gave Farid a giant hug that lifted him off the ground. We enjoyed a laugh on Farid.

Farid kept his black beard very short for business—unlike Shah's whose growth fast-approached his waist.

"How's business, Yosif? I heard from several friends about your recent troubles," I said.

"I'm weary from having to deal with all the crap these communists have brought about! The rubbish of the Soviet invasion has caused a lot of people in the jewel business to be careless and sloppy."

Shah broke into the conversation. "Yosif, I heard you were written up in the local newspaper last week. What was the commotion all about?"

I intervened. "Do you mind, Yosif?"

"All right, go ahead." Yosif rolled his eyes.

"It's not what happened to Yosif, it's what happened to a Pakistani who tried to stiff him," I said. "Several weeks ago, Yosif tracked down a jewel agent's runner who owed him quite a bit of money on some stones he advanced on credit. The guy tried to skip out without paying him his share after selling the jewels. The runner's boss said he knew nothing about it. So when Yosif caught up with the runner in India, he cut off his ear and sent it in the mail to his boss. The boss got the message, all right, and paid Yosif right away—with interest."

"My God," said Farid.

"Sometimes such extremes are necessary," said Yosif.

A moment of silence followed, but was soon broken, when Sher walked into the darkroom from the studio's small kitchen with a silver platter, bearing a large, steaming teapot and cups for everyone. After Sher served us, he and Shah briefly teased each other about who had the longest and fullest beard between them. The rest of us enjoyed a good laugh. Afterwards, Sher told everyone how glad he was to see us together again, and departed back to the front studio.

"How is business with you, Farid?" Yosif said, striking

back up our conversion.

"Well, like you, this horrible war has affected my operations. My main business is taking large groups of well-to-do Afghan refugees to Pakistan or India and then, personally escorting them to Europe. From there, many of them go on to settle in the United States.

"But things have changed. Due to the large influx of immigrants from this area, the American government has put the screws to the Pakistan consulate. The constant pressure has forced the Pakistani government to give in. In turn, they have put restrictions on all scheduled westbound flights from the Karachi International airport. They are making it very difficult for me to get the proper tickets and passports for my clients' passage. It's costing me a lot of serious money. Oh well, that's the breaks." Farid grinned.

"Farid, you always have that silly smirk on your fat face, even when things are really bad," said Shah, throwing up his arms in despair. "You need to take a more serious look at life!"

Farid laughed out loud.

Yosif smiled.

Shah fumed.

I stepped in at this point. "Gentlemen, that's why we're here. I have a fabulous plan that can help us all out!"

Several hours later, after I'd gone over the details of the operation, every person gave their input and everyone nodded "yes," together.

We overwhelmingly felt the elated unity needed to cement this risky operation. Though everyone had slightly different motivations for their commitment, we all looked forward to success—despite the ugliness of the war.

CHAPTER 5

The Plan

*W*e would have to wait at least three months before late summer arrived, when the frozen ground along the Kyber Pass region would be thawed out enough for us to trench out even a few shallow holes to retrieve the jewels. In the meantime, there were plenty of preparations to be made regarding the procurement of the proper weapons and surveillance equipment we needed to handle the job right.

Getting around in Peshawar proved difficult at first. My entire body reeled from the barbaric torture, courtesy of those Afghan communist hoodlums. Constant pain plagued me, and the pain killers had no effect unless I opted to swallow enough to put me out—which I couldn't do and still stay alert on the streets.

Yosif met with Stella in Peshawar, within days of our meeting at Sher's. He telephoned me that afternoon to relate that our plans had impressed her and she would handle two aspects of the mission: contact Yosif's buyers in Korea to meet us in Bangkok and pre-purchase the necessary airline tickets needed to flee Peshawar to the Pakistan border town of Lahore. We decided to have all three of us meet the next morning at the studio, to lay out the particulars.

After breakfast, just as I took my last sip of tea, my nephew bolted through the door to get me.

"Abdul, Abdul, your friends are here!" he blurted out.

Elated to the news, my heart pounded as I limped over to the studio in anticipation of seeing Stella after all these years. I swung open the back door to find Stella and Yosif studying some of Sher's photography by the print dryer.

"Stella, how good to see you!"

"Abdul, how are you dear?"

"I'm still breathing, as you can see. It's so good to see you again."

We embraced and laughed. Her beautiful, shoulder-length blonde hair smelled of a fresh spring bouquet.

Stella looked prettier than ever. She had developed into a lovely woman. Lean and tan, her cheerful hazel eyes shown brightly. High cheek bones and thin, yet, well-defined lips still inspirited an aristocratic air about her. She wore little makeup—never needed it since we first met.

"Abdul, how do feel, really? You look very tired."

"I'm doing okay, considering what the communists put me through. I'm tired of the pain. But, mentally, I'm fairing well. I did have nightmares, but I'm sleeping better now."

I turned to Yosif. "Stella looks marvelous."

Yosif smiled widely. "The best looking woman, and one of the brightest on the continent."

"Oh, you men." She winked. "Thank you very much for the compliments. Except for the leers and whistles, compliments are hard to get around this town. The women aren't exactly crazy about me being an American and running around the streets, either."

"They are just jealous," Yosif said, with a big smile.

"Probably so. Don't know if it's my American looks, the freedom we Western women have, or the politics of the war. Most likely, a bit of everything."

"Nevertheless, you're beautiful. Not only on the outside, but from the inside too," Yosif said.

"Thank you." She leaned over and gave Yosif a soft kiss on his cheek.

Yosif turned a little red. He wasn't accustomed to open affection from a woman.

Stella smiled. "Now, tell me about these marvelous

jewels, Abdul."

"They're incredible. I would guess there are thirty, maybe forty cut stones—a lot of emeralds and a selection of rubies and sapphires, approximately two to four carats each. Plus, there are at least a half a dozen larger-sized rubies as big as my thumbnail, encased in rock. Yosif and I guess that the whole lot could be worth several million American dollars, possibly more."

"We're hoping for close to that amount," said Yosif. "I'll have a better idea when I see them. The Koreans are tough. They take negotiations to an absurd level. But they're willing to travel to meet us. They're just hours away by air from Bangkok. Their group can come and go out of Bangkok without any visas or paperwork. It's a necessary convenience we need on this job."

"Yes. What have you and Stella figured out?" I asked.

"We have laid out the cities and airports we need to go through to insure smooth travel all the way there. Abdul, when you, Shah, and Farid come back across the border with the jewels, Stella will have tickets waiting for all four of us at Will Call at the Peshawar airport. I'll be there an hour before your arrival to make sure everything is handled with the proper authorities."

"Great. One question though. Stella, what if it takes longer than we've plan to recover the jewels at the fort, and arrive back a day or two late?"

"No problem. Since I'm an American, I can make reservations for all of you, under fictitious American names. If you don't arrive on the day planned, I'll call to apologize for our party not showing up because of a postponed business meeting, and book the same flight for the next day. They won't suspect anything. The airport officials are used to us

Westerners making reservations all the time and canceling at the last minute—especially us women." She tossed her hair back in jest.

"There's really no problem," Yosif said. "The planes are never even close to being full in August."

"Good! What about the rest of our trip?" I tapped my fingers on the metal photo-developing tray next to me.

"Just like we discussed several days ago. After we arrive at Lahore, we will take a short cab ride to the Pakistan-Indian border to cross over by foot. It should go smoothly, since Farid knows most of the guards and officials there. He always carries a big bundle of American currency, which puts a smile on any official's face. Once across the border, we'll hire a car to drive us to Amritsar to catch a quick plane to Delhi. Hopefully there won't be any snags—but you never know in this insane war."

Stella interjected. "If I don't hear from you gentlemen by early evening, back here at my hotel, I'll assume everything went fine getting out of Pakistan, and will call Yosif's contacts in Korea, telling them to meet us the next evening in Bangkok. I will then take a 6:30 flight from Peshawar to Karachi and immediately hop on a late flight to Bangkok. I'll greet you men the next day when you finally fly into Bangkok from Delhi."

"Yes, exactly," Yosif said. "Abdul, on the evening the four of us stay over in Delhi, we will meet with Farid's Sikh contact there, who will arrange for our forged passports and visas to be prepared in Old Delhi. The next morning we pick up our documentation and fly into Bangkok to rendezvous with Stella for our meeting with the Koreans that evening."

"Excellent!" I said. I gave both Farid and Stella big hugs; that is, as much as my body could manage to give.

"We have to go now," said Yosif. "We have other business to attend to."

"Abdul, it's really great to see you again. It has been such a long time," Stella said.

"Yes, too long," I said. We gave each other a kiss on the cheek. "See you soon. Where are you staying, Stella, here close?"

Stella and Yosif broke out in laughter. Yosif placed his arm gently around her shoulder. "A favorite place of yours." He winked. "The old Green Hotel."

"Really?" I replied. "Stella, when did you move in?"

"Yesterday. I'll be staying for at least a month."

"Maybe I'll meet you and Yosif there for dinner next week. I can fill you in on how Shah, Farid and I are doing with provisioning our mission into Afghanistan."

"Sounds like a plan." Stella's dimples embraced her lovely smile.

Yosif came over to me, put his large hand on my shoulder, and whispered into my ear: "Once you get back across the border, don't worry about a thing. I'll make sure that nothing happens to you. Try to rest as much as possible."

On their way out, Yosif and Stella stopped in the adjoining parlor of the studio to compliment Sher on his photography. As they left through the front door, I saw them exchange glances with starry eyes. They had fallen in love.

CHAPTER 6

Bordertown

*A*ugust's deadline left me less than three months to get my team ready for the trip back to the PDPA Fort for the jewels. We chose the times and places to purchase all the necessary arms needed to pull off our mission: mine detector; night-vision glasses; and remote person-to-person communications. The operation's success depended upon as much secrecy as possible, especially since they had me being watched for clues to both the location and the time for retrieving the jewels.

To confuse the smugglers, I made an airline reservation for July to return to New York to be with my wife until August rolled around. Over two years had passed since I had seen Laila, and I was anxious to see her. I looked forward to a two-month rest—good for both my marriage, as well as my battered mind and body.

In preparation for our trip back into Afghanistan, we needed to search out light machine guns and ammo in the notorious Bordertown, located right in middle of the Free Zone. It ran parallel to the Afghan-Pakistani border thirty kilometers to either side, which made it the perfect place to purchase what we wanted for our mission, and still remain anonymous.

Various border tribes of Pashtun descent resided in this small crude town—mostly Afridis, known for their independence and fierce fighting capabilities. The Pashtun tribes living on either side of Afghanistan or Pakistan, all had strong family ties with most other villages throughout the Free Zone. None of the various border tribes claimed allegiance to either country. The Afridis' bonded only with their own extended families. Their idea of creature comforts came from a Coleman lantern to light the men's discussion groups at night.

The first Saturday in May, as scheduled, Farid and Shah picked me up a few streets down from Sher's studio. Farid came speeding up in a shiny, black '75 Range Rover, and slammed on the brakes. A cloud of dust engulfed the entire side of the road. As it dissipated, Farid and Shah laughed hysterically.

"You guys are crazy!"

"Ready for a leisurely jaunt in the country, Abdul?" asked the grinning Farid.

"Talk about drawing attention to ourselves," I replied.

"Don't worry, everything is under control. Get in."

Before I barely got seated in the back, he floored the accelerator. The locals walking down either side of the street scurried in all directions, half of them shouting and gesturing angrily at us.

"Are you nuts?" I yelled. I shot a look at Shah who cowered. Farid slapped his free hand on the dashboard, and shouted, "Whooo!—you handle well. Whooo, baby!"

I've got a problem here. Farid still has a lot of child in him. I'm going to have to watch his antics to make sure he doesn't draw attention to us throughout the mission.

Farid reached over and grabbed me with his free hand. "We're heading across town to the Chawk Yadgar Square to pick up some fruit and water. We can walk around the bazaar for a while to lose any possible tails. The central square will be jammed. I can easily shake them in the traffic with this baby underneath me. When we head out for Bordertown, no one will be behind us. So, relax. You worry too much."

"Relax? I'll relax when you slow this thing down. This car and your driving are kind of an ostentatious display of wealth, don't you think? By the way, how did you get your hands on this Rover?"

"I bought it several months ago on the black market, just over the Indian border near Lahore."

Shah turned around and said, "I think it's real nice. Look at the leather seats and mahogany paneling throughout. Farid did get a good deal on it—he paid only $12,000 American dollars. A steal for this area. Don't you agree?"

"Sure," I said. "Here you guys are living in the middle of the carnapping capital of the world, and you're driving one of the most expensive rides in town like you're a European race car driver. Great thinking."

"Ahhh, don't be so pessimistic," Farid said, grinning. "Besides, the families that steal luxury cars for money in Peshawar all know me. I do them favors all the time, and they treat me with respect. The Rover's safe."

"You like to push everything to the limit," I replied.

"Why not? You only live once," said Shah. "By the way, you should talk. You're the one who got us involved in this whole damned crazy jewel game in the first place."

They laughed and slapped each other on the back. I smiled. "Fine, fine. You got me. But, please, Farid, try to drive a little slower for my sake. All right? Please?"

"Sure, until we leave the square. Then, should there be any of those gangster clowns following us, I'll probably drive like Andretti."

"Just don't get us in a wreck," I said.

"Sit back, relax. Enjoy some comfort, courtesy of the English," Farid said.

When we arrived in the old part of the city, bumper-to-bumper traffic jammed the Chawk Yadgar bazaar's streets. Drivers cut in and out of the small streets like blind madmen. People on the streets needed eyes behind their heads just to survive.

It was the main shopping day for the locals. New York at rush hour looked tame compared to this motorized riot of diesel Toyota and Nissan pickups, Toyota Camrys, and Russian Jeeps pitted against throngs of the local Pashtuns and Afghan refugees with their mules and camels.

The Afghan men, many Mujahidin taking a short break from the hell, strode through the streets with black and white turbans crowning their heads. The end of the turban's cloth draped over the lower part of their faces. The local Peshawar men sported multi-colored turbans. The women—both Pakistani and Afghan—wore long, ankle-length pastel colored, muslin dresses. They used their Chadris to veil themselves from the top of their heads down, with only eyes and brows showing through.

Most of the shops were small, narrow one-storied buildings, several hundred years old, made of timber, stone and mud. Outside the front entrance, the storekeepers displayed samples of their goods, with the finer merchandise for consideration inside. The square swelled with: fresh produce stores; leather merchants selling bandoleers, hats and holsters; brass and copper pot merchants; dealers of Pashtun tribal jewelry—mainly silver and semi-precious stones; and a host of money-changers and letter writers who commanded every crook available within the walls.

We finally worked our way over, after parking in a small alley behind a brass and copper wares shop owned by a friend of Shah's. He expected us and, all morning, his twin boys held the parking spot for us. Farid tipped each one with a five dollar bill as soon as he stepped down out of the Rover. The eight-year-old boys jumped into the air, letting out a gleeful shout of thanks. Within seconds, they disappeared into the bazaar.

After a quick thanks to Shah's friend, we took off on foot into the crowded sea of humanity. Only a foreigner of different color or height, prompted scrutiny—although heated bartering drew attention.

During our walk, we intermittently stopped to argue about anything that came to mind—just to see if anyone either developed a pattern of pausing to glance our way, or followed behind at a safe distance.

At a huge fruit stand, frequented by Farid and Shah, the farmers has piled stacks of fruit baskets—six to seven feet high—in makeshift, free-standing shelves. The baskets contained: red and orange apples, yellow pears, watermelons, bananas, lemons, kumquats, pomegranates, and figs. In addition, a large array of various-sized potatoes, corn, garlic, shallots and onions filled other baskets. The freshly-picked fruit filled the air with a delightful fragrance. My stomach growled and my mouth watered in anticipation of sinking my teeth into a ripe, juicy pear.

I selected a few choice pears and apples for our trip, and Shah bought several small bottles of ice cold spring water. We took a different route back to the Rover, and, luckily, no one followed us.

As Farid drove out of the Chawk Yadgar Square, Shah and I kept a close look for any possible tails.

We headed out the west end of Peshawar within a half an hour, and drove down the main highway. Farid toned down his aggressive driving to a slow roar, I'm sure for my benefit. I stretched out between the two back seats to relax, and before I dozed off to sleep, I noticed him smiling at me in approval through the rearview mirror.

Two hours later, we arrived at the edge of Bordertown.

The warm weather, typical for this time of year, had us down to our short-sleeved shirts—though the ground would still be frozen for several more months.

Driving in this small, barren, hilly town reminded me of the TV shows I'd seen, about riding into Anchorage during the Gold Rush days of the 1800s. Since every man in Bordertown carried a weapon, an unarmed man would portray the tenderfoot city slicker—an out-of-place buffoon on American westerns, the laughing stock of the entire town.

Accompanied by the Mujahidin, I had purchased weapons here, several times. The bazaar streets provided the only action.

Four streets ran parallel to each other, with tall wood-framed structures on each side. As I walked through the entrance, I noted narrow stalls lined up against each other—on both sides of the street—all roofed with three-foot-high cement floors to keep the merchandise dry during the monsoon season. It had a barn-like feel, except for the lack of a roof extending over the street itself.

"We'll park the beast on the rear side by the open barbecue pits where there is plenty of room," Farid said with a large smile.

"Great idea," I replied.

Shah turned around and chuckled. "It will be a lot easier and safer. We don't want to scare the dickens out of an arms dealer we might possibly want to bargain with, now would we?"

"You guys don't trust me!" Farid burst out in laughter.

We grinned like crazy.

"I know Shah comes here a lot for the resistance. But, Farid, you've been here a lot of times too?"

"Yes, many times. As you know, they don't only sell arms

here. They have an excellent selection of black market refrigerators, air conditioners, microwaves, televisions, fax machines, and other fancy electronic stuff nearly impossible to obtain in Pakistan, without paying stiff licensing fees. I buy stuff here all the time—not only for my family, but for my business clients and friends."

"Let's grab something to eat before it gets too hot. I'll buy," Shah said. "Park on the northwest side at the far corner. There's a family there that makes a great Shish kabob."

Farid nodded. "I know the place. They serve a delicious beef stew as well."

Farid hit the accelerator as he drove around the bazaar, but I didn't care. My stomached growled in anticipation of savory pieces of lamb and beef. I too had eaten there before, and the lamb kabob was the best around.

We jumped out of the Rover and grabbed our rifles from the back of the vehicle. Each of us also had a side arm.

The enticing aroma of the wood-charcoal barbecues filled the air. We found one table left with an awning and grabbed it.

Shah took our rifles, and walked out several yards away, and propped up our three rifles into a free-standing teepee. All of the other customers did the same thing, and, like them, we kept our side arms with us.

Our waiter came over to take our order of Kabobs, beef stew, and cold Pepsis.

The sky was clear except for high, waning stratospheric clouds. A few flies swarmed around our table, but not too bad for this time of year. I had seen it much worse, in late summer, in other, more congested, bazaars.

"Farid!" Someone called out from a nearby table. Farid looked over and seemed to recognize the man right away.

"It's good to see you again," the man said as he got up from his table of friends and came over to where we sat. "Have you come to buy some appliances for your friends?"

Farid introduced us. Sabor, a popular trader of air conditioners and refrigerators in town, in his late forties, wore expensive silk robes and fine jewelry.

"We actually don't have many plans for today," Farid said. "The three of us just decided to take a ride to get out of Peshawar for the day, and relax. Might pick up a few things. Anything exciting going on in Bordertown?"

"Well, the Pakistani border patrol came out yesterday to inspect the fort of a local gunrunner and drug supplier, to see if there were any illegal guns or drugs. The government always gives the local tribes in the Free Zone three days notice, by law, before searching any house or fort. The family being searched—in this case the Wasi family—always has plenty of time to store their contraband somewhere else before the authorities can conduct the search. It's rather pointless to even go through the charade, but they always do. As soon as the government officials leave town, they haul the contraband right back into the fort again. Quite a bureaucratic show, yes?"

We laughed.

"I've done business with the Wasi family once before," Shah said. "They're clever people." .

Sabor nodded in agreement. "I agree. Anyway to celebrate yesterday's futile search at the fort, the Wasi's had a big barbecue for their family and immediate cousins last night shortly after the officials' Jeeps headed out of town. I heard it was quite a get-together.

"They own one of the largest forts here in the area— located just outside this edge of town. In fact, it's one of the forts you can see from here. Look over there on top of the high bluff to your right."

He continued, "The three-storied fort, built on the highest bluff overlooking the bazaar is said to have three major courtyards within the walls, and close to a dozen houses inside. I hear it's magnificently furnished for the extended families who live there."

When our waiter brought our meal, Sabor politely excused himself and went back to join his friends.

The lamb, marinated overnight in a spicy blend of herbs and local citrus juices, looked tasty. The cook slid off the meat directly onto a flat piece of Naan bread—very similar to Armenian pita bread—making a sandwich of sorts. After our first bites and compliments, no one said anything. We just ate.

The waiter soon followed with two large bowls of piping-hot beef and potato stew. We each took a piece of Naan from a pile of bread he had thrown down on the center of the table and tore it up into small pieces, placing the bread into the bottom of the individual serving bowls set on the table. In turn, we spooned the stew's beef, potatoes and juices over the top of the torn bread. To eat the stew, we used additional pieces of bread to scoop up the favorable mixture. Everything was hot and delicious.

After we finished our satisfying meal and paid the bill, we gathered our rifles to head into the bazaar to check out the weapons available. We had come today to purchase weapons, not take them home with us.

Shah went over the plan again. "If we strike a deal with someone today, Farid's men will pick up the weapons at least a few days later at the seller's fort or home, preferably at night. Right?"

"Yes, of course," said Farid. "In fact, my men are coming

through this area to smuggle some people out of Afghanistan next weekend. They will pick up the weapons here and drop them off at your cousin's farm on the way to Kabul for safe-keeping. There shouldn't be any problems. What are their names again?"

"Kheir Hammad and his son, Ghulam," Shah proudly said. "They have agreed to hide our weapons and equipment at their farm until we go in. They considered our invitation to join us for the actual operation, and they're in. It's perfect. Not only is their village, Noar-A-Amir, a few hours away, by foot, from the jewels, but the farm is also a perfect place for us to stay the day before we go in at night. That way, in case we can't find the jewels the first night, we can go back to their village for the day to rest before the next evening's attempt."

"Excellent," I said. "Just what we hoped for, two weeks ago. Let's find some light machine guns first. Buying them won't draw that much attention around here."

In Bordertown, you could trust the dealers with your money. Their reputations depended upon it. We traveled through the crowded bazaar and stopped by dealers with whom Shah and I were familiar. The heavy feeling of eating the large afternoon meal soon dissipated.

We finally negotiated a purchase of three light machine guns, ironically, from the Wasi family. The weapons they showed us were all right, but we wanted better guns—so we offered more American dollars to get better quality arms we could depend upon not to jam in a firefight.

They said a new supply that we would be happy with would arrive in the next day or two. Farid agreed to have his men stop by the following Sunday to pick up the weapons. Everything was agreed and shook upon. For the next hour, we strolled through the bazaar and leisurely picked up a few items to bring back with us, for friends.

We drove home to Peshawar in the late afternoon. No one suspected anything of our plans for the guns. With the machine guns off our list, next I would need to locate a decent mine detector, night vision glasses and communications equipment in Holland, on the way back to New York.

Content with the mission's success to date, I enjoyed the drive back into Peshawar, even with Farid behind the wheel.

CHAPTER 7

Abroad until August

*T*he time came for me to go home to Laila. But, first I had to fly to the Netherlands.

What I thought would be an easy trip out of Pakistan turned into crap when I flew into Karachi International Airport to catch my flight to Frankfurt.

I entered the terminal lounge area from the airfield entrance in a casual manner. Just as I walked in, a heavily-built, nearly bald, Pakistani man in his early fifties, dressed in a suit and tie, stood twenty feet directly ahead of me. He stared at me with a shit-eating grin on his fat face. Right behind him stood two uniformed airport guards with no smiles whatsoever. They toted machine guns.

Damn! One of the jewel dealer's men must have spotted me at the Peshawar airport and phoned ahead to their contacts in Karachi.

As I approached them, the man in the suit pulled out his wallet and flashed a badge in my face.

"Mr. Barkzi, we've been expecting you. Welcome to Karachi. I'm Inspector Rashid from Customs. We got an anonymous call you might be carrying some illegal contraband. We need to check you and your luggage. Please, follow me."

Within a half-hour they seated me butt naked on a cold steel chair, in a small eight-by-ten room. Bright fluorescent lights glared down, and the contents of my two suitcases lay spewed all over the floor in front of me. The guards had torn apart the lining from clothing, and dissected my toiletry items, including the toothpaste, to see if anything concealed precious stones.

"All right, it appears that you're clean," Rashid said, in a dubious tone. "Now get dressed and get the hell out of here."

His condescending smirk made me grit my teeth, as he walked out the door.

Fuck you!

I dressed quickly, threw my belongings into my luggage, and ran to the international boarding gates.

Fortunately, the connecting plane to Frankfort had arrived an hour late, and I made my flight.

I fumed, during the long flight into Frankfurt. Those bastards must have known I didn't have the jewels on me. They only wanted to intimidate me. By the time I made my connecting flight into Amsterdam, I finally cooled my head.

From all the countries I'd visited on business trips or holidays, the Netherlands won out as the country of anything goes. Amsterdammers rarely lacked tolerance.

Shah had given me two arms-dealers phone numbers to call as soon as I arrived at the airport. They had a good track record, for the Mujahidin had dealt with them on almost a monthly basis. I would purchase what we needed under the auspices of transacting a regular business deal, to draw off any possible questions in regards to the use of the specific equipment we needed. Besides they knew not to ask many questions—simply as a matter of course.

In late morning I landed in the modern Schiphol Airport, eight kilometers southwest of Amsterdam. An assistant of the first dealer's answered the phone and informed me that his employer had left the city to handle some unexpected, urgent business, and would not return for several more days. I politely informed him that my plans kept me in Amsterdam for only a day or two. Had I not found what we needed in the next few days, I would call back.

I did reach the second dealer, and he invited me over to his home, located along the prized Reguliersgracht canal on the Eastern ring, originally dug out during the late 1600's. I took the train from the air terminal into Amsterdam's Central Station and, from there, hired a cab to head straight over to his place in the canals, west of the station. The last leg, two kilometers, took more than an hour, due to the vast amount of bicycle traffic utilizing the privileged right-of-way in the city. A definite reversal from the rules of the road in Pakistan.

The immediate splendor of the Reguliersgracht canal took me by surprise. The amber leaves on the trees, along both banks, gently floated down in handfuls and came to rest on the water. I arrived at the dealer's home, one of several built side by side amongst a narrow street of houses. I marveled at it's exterior, lavishly adorned with detailed wood craftsmanship along the shutters and eaves. A large joint outdoor patio dock graced the bank of the canal. Tied up alongside, a classic, all-mahogany Chris Craft swayed gently in the water. The early-fifties, vintage model appeared to have the maintenance that only tender loving care could have provided over the years.

The motor boat captains in Venice would drool over this gem.

I lifted a giant seashell-shaped brass knocker and let it fall on the front door of the elegant, five-story house. Step gables crowned the top of the building, to complete it's magnificent Dutch-Renaissance style. It would seem, the arms dealer, Mr. Michel Mor, had done very well for himself.

A tall, blond-haired, blue-eyed man, in his middle forties, opened the door and stepped onto the front porch. He extended his long, muscular hand to greet me.

"Abdul, welcome to Amsterdam, the city of international brotherly love. My instructions must have been adequate—you got here in good time." Michel had a deep, warm voice, and a genuine, friendly smile. He shook my hand firmly.

"Michel, it's a pleasure to meet you."

"Please forget the formalities of calling me Michel. You can call me Mike. You know, like the nickname they always use in the United States." He winked. "Shah told me a little about you. You have a wife waiting for you back in America. You must be anxious to get home to her, eh?"

"Yes, very much so. It's been over two years, now. A long time."

"Ah, yes. Well, welcome to my home. Let's go to the back garden," he said, and showed me inside. "I will get my son, Storm—who by the way, is now my new business partner. I would like you to meet him. He's only twenty-two, still a little wet behind the ears, but he has guts. That's what it takes in this crazy business."

As we walked through the house, I stared at the Dutch antiques which filled every available spot along the walls. We walked outside to the porch through huge, four-paneled Dutch doors.

"Please sit down and enjoy these new comfortable, wicker chairs that just arrived from Jakarta. Storm is on the phone upstairs. I'll tell him you are here and have him bring some drinks. A cocktail? A beer?"

"No thank you. Though, something cold would be nice. A soda—Pepsi?"

"Sure. It's almost five-o'clock—time to relax." He grinned. "You don't mind if I imbibe in some local Dutch Gin do you? Our Genever is very good."

"Of course not," I assured him. "By the way, you have a beautiful home and view. The ambiance is overwhelming."

"Thank you. Enjoy. I'll be right back."

I took in the surrounding back patio. The yard was huge for a canal house, with a finely manicured lawn, various perfectly-pruned dwarf fruit trees, and a large water fountain that spanned at least fifteen feet across, with marble swans afloat in the center.

Beautiful.

A few minutes later, Mike came back through the garden door with his son right behind him. Storm's strapping, muscular physique matched his father's.

"Abdul, I would like to introduce my son, Storm."

"Welcome to Amsterdam," said Storm in a husky voice.

"Thank you. You look just like your father."

"Yes, everyone says the same thing. My full-time involvement in the business now has everyone joking. When they see us coming, they hoot, 'Here come the Moors, run for your lives!'

Mike chuckled. "We keep telling our suppliers and customers that we provide the arms only to conquer invaders, not actually use them."

I laughed politely with them.

"Well, I'm going for the drinks," said Storm. "It's a Pepsi, right?"

"Please," I said.

When Storm left to get the drinks, Mike said, "Tell me, how are things going for the resistance? Good, I hope?"

"Things could be better, but we are holding our own. It's going to be a long war. We're hoping that after a year or two, pressure from the West will be on Moscow to finally bow out. They already know they have made a big mistake trying to control us. History is on our side. Remember, Alexander the Great could only conquer Afghanistan, but never hold her. He even gave in and took an Afghan woman as his bride—leaving our country in peace. Yes, Afghanistan is becoming the Soviets' own special Vietnam war."

"I hope you kick the bastard Ruskies out. The sooner they come to grips with this being a no-win situation for them, the better."

"They will—we will prevail." I paused for a moment, then smiling said, "But, Mike, that will be a lot less business for you,"

"Don't worry, there will be another conflict somewhere in the world to come along and replace it." Mike smiled back.

Storm reappeared with the drinks.

We touched our drinks in salute.

"Well, Abdul. Would you like to take a peek inside the Chris Craft we have tied up on our dock?" asked Mike. "Its a real beauty inside, and there's some items on board I think might interest you personally."

"Sure, I can't wait to see the boat."

We headed back out to the canal, where we finished our drinks on their outdoor dock patio and took in the pleasant atmosphere along the canal. The three of us climbed aboard the Chris Craft and went directly below. Mike was right about the warm, rich teakwood interior; but, more importantly, on the port side, laying on the seat cushion—I eyed a valuable find: a French made, wireless communications package; three night-vision glasses from Britain; and an older Canadian made, explosive-ordinance detector.

I let out a shout of glee.

"Just what the cook ordered, eh, Abdul?" said Mike.

He and Storm chuckled kindly.

"Yes, everything we need, except we actually need only three headsets."

"I knew that, but I have quite a few laying around in one

of our canal warehouses, so I threw it in for good measure."

"Thank you!"

"No problem. The price will be the same as I told Shah over the phone last week—eight thousand American dollars. Is that O.K.?"

"Yes, fine, fine. Everything looks in great shape. I will call Shah this evening and have him wire the money to your Swiss account, as agreed to before."

"It's a deal then. Have Shah call me in a few days to arrange the shipping from here to Karachi."

"With pleasure."

Storm picked up the mine detector.

"My son knows how to use this stuff blindfolded," boasted Mike. "Listen, Abdul, after you and Storm go over everything, would you like to join us for an excellent meal this evening? We would like to take you to the Sama Sebo— they have the best selection of authentic Indonesian food on this continent."

"It sounds great, but as you know, I haven't seen my wife, Laila, for over two years. There are some seats left on this evening's flight to Frankfurt International, where I can hop a flight to New York."

They smiled at each other.

"Maybe the next time you and Laila come to Amsterdam on holiday, you'll give us a ring, and we'll go then."

"You're on."

"Great! Well, Abdul, its been a pleasure doing business with you. I'll let Storm show you the equipment. Have a good trip home."

Mike shook my hand firmly again.

He's a good man.

After Storm instructed me on how to use the gear, he

took me to the airport to catch the last evening flight to Frankfurt. I couldn't have enjoyed dinner anyway. My stomach felt knotted thinking about seeing Laila, in only nine hours.

*   *   *

The plane banked for final approach to Kennedy International. In fifteen minutes I would embrace my dear Laila. As the wing levers made their synchronized moves for landing, my mind raced back to when we first met.

The call that put me in contact with the love of my life came one evening when I had my best friend in college, Richard, and his parents, Jerry and Elaine Stein, over for dinner. Jerry had helped me get my interview with The Broadway theater the summer I graduated and, that night, we celebrated the first anniversary of my hiring.

As honor students in business college together, Richard and I hit it off right away. Because of his Jewish heritage and my nationality, both of us faced racial abuse from the majority of the people crossing our paths in school—even in Manhattan.

Jerry and Elaine took me in as their second son, and I stayed with them many times while attending college. They were people of great heart and courage—good people, and steadfast to their own Jewish culture and faith.

My sister-in-law, then a student at the University of Indianapolis, called me up to say that her sister Laila would be flying in to the United States the next evening to visit her, for several weeks. She asked if I'd spend some time with her at the airport during her brief layover.

After I got off the phone and relayed the news, Elaine

said instinctively, "Abdul, I think you have just received a Godsend." To this day I wonder how she could know this.

I arrived at the airport the next evening to learn that the airlines had canceled Laila's connecting flight to Indiana.

When I first saw her come off the plane, I knew that dating American girls had been a poor substitute for what I wanted. I had a lot of fun, but the commonalty of an Afghan woman provided me what I needed to be complete. As I talked to her I realized that her sweet disposition, yet independent mind, was exactly what I had yearned for. She seemed attracted to me. Her eyes danced with mine. My stomach had the proverbial butterflies. We were the perfect match.

Throughout that evening, and until the break of dawn, I drove her all over Manhattan. She responded like a kid visiting Disneyland for the first time. That morning when I put her on the plane, her energetic nature overcame her sleepless night. The following week I visited her at the Indianapolis campus and, the day before she left to return to Afghanistan, I proposed marriage. It caught her by surprise but, after a minute she accepted with tears of joy; however her parents in Afghanistan had to approve. Three weeks later she came back to me in the United States with a box of chocolates in hand—our people's way of signifying that her parents had given their consent, which also married us, by Afghan Muslim law. Laila and I tied the knot legally, for Uncle Sam, the next day at the Courthouse, with Richard, Jerry, and Elaine as our witnesses.

*   *   *

The miraculous phone call from my sister-in-law, so many years ago, made a great difference in my life. The plane made a final turn before starting its descent, and with it, my thoughts returned to the present.

My heart pounded wildly as I walked down the gateway to the concourse. She stood right up front when I walked out into the waiting lounge. Laila looked like an angel. She hadn't aged a day in my mind since I left to join the resistance, and in fact, she looked younger than when I left her over two years ago. I had no idea what she would think of my worn and hardened looks.

"Abdul! Abdul!" she laughed, with tears streaming down her face. She ran to me with arms wide open, clutching a single red rose in one hand. Her hazel eyes sparkled like diamonds.

"You look great." My voice cracked. "I'm so glad to be home with you." I embraced her and lifted her off the ground.

Laila had let her hair grow, in my absence. It fell to her waist. Blue jeans and an oversized blue workshirt adorned her 5'-3" petite frame.

"Let's go into town and have dinner at the Darwesh Restaurant. They have several private booths," I said.

"Yes, Oh yes. That would be nice—then, we'll go straight home."

"Of course, my lovely." I smiled like a love-smitten teenager.

The Darwesh, located in SoHo—an upbeat neighborhood of artists and people of all races and creeds—had been my hangout since college. The restaurant became Laila's favorite, too, when we got married.

When we walked in, the maitre d' gave us big hugs, and welcomed me back home. He immediately put us in a cozy booth in the back corner, out of sight and earshot of the other tables.

"My dear, wonderful, husband. You are home, at last with me," she said, softly. "Every night you were gone, I snuggled up with my pillow and thought of holding you close, dear. I missed you so much. Please tell me you'll never go back to the resistance. I couldn't bear the pain again." Laila's eyes swelled with tears. "When they told me you had been tortured, I went absolutely crazy. Tell me you'll never put yourself in danger any more. Please."

"Laila, I missed you. I've left the CIA for good and I have gone on my last mission for the Mujahidin. No more war."

"Thank you, thank you." She wiped the tears away from her eyes.

I took her hands in one of mine and wiped away a long tear she missed. "I'm sorry I left you alone, but I had to go. It would have eaten me alive to stay home with those communists killing our families and people. You did understand, didn't you?"

"Many times I did not. Could you have really made a difference? I hoped that you really didn't think you could turn back the clock for the people of Afghanistan?"

"I never thought I could restore our old country back to the way it was, but, did I make a difference? Yes, I made a difference. At least at first, until the Jehad turned into a war of greed on both sides."

"So, risking your life wasn't in vain, Dear?"

"Of course not. Sooner or later the Russians will be forced to leave our country. They are losing innocent Russian sons over there. The Soviet leaders now know they can't rule our people. It's just a matter of time."

I rubbed the top of her soft, left hand. Her diamond ring glittered like a small bonfire—it warmed my heart.

"I love you, Abdul. Please stay home with me now."

"I'll love you always," I said softly. A small tear slowly fell down my cheek.

She wiped it away from my face, and smiled.

My two-month stay with Laila in Manhattan was heaven. During our afternoon walks in Central Park, we would enjoy a large slice of cheese pizza together—the kind Joe dreamed about, back in Peshawar. During the evenings, I took her to our favorite hangouts downtown in the Village. We enjoyed romantic candlelight dinners and live entertainment at several Moroccan and Afghan nightclubs that we had frequented when we first dated. We got together with old friends and had a great time—though she preferred not to socialize too long, wanting to stay close to me to make up for lost time.

To finally get away by ourselves, we took off to upstate New York to a private mountain cabin that belonged to the Steins. While I was away, Laila had gotten her drivers license. It helped keep her mind off my absence. She got a real kick out of sharing the driving responsibility up into the mountains.

We had a lovely, quiet time while getting to know each other all over again. When we weren't doing something together, she insisted that I try to rest as much as possible. My mind and body became whole again.

Before I knew it, the two months had passed. During the entire time, I didn't mention anything about the jewels, not wanting to ruin our brief time together. Hearing the details of my torture, had already upset her and I didn't want her to worry about me for the several weeks I would be gone. Her vivid imagination, along with her extreme sensitivity, would have her crying herself to sleep, thinking of what might be happening to me.

It was hard to get on the plane to go back for the jewels, especially since I hadn't told Laila the whole story. I said there was unfinished business I needed to handle in Europe and Pakistan for the resistance. I also promised her that, while in Peshawar, I would make the final arrangements with Farid to smuggle out my brother's family. Tears filled her eyes the half hour before I boarded the plane at Kennedy International Airport. I could hardly hold back my emotions, and bit my bottom lip to hold my composure. As I walked through the ramp door, it felt as if my stomach dropped to my knees. I blew her a final kiss good-bye.

I'll see you soon, my love.

*　*　*

The first flight took me into Frankfurt, Germany. Yosif had flown over a month earlier for a little rest and relaxation—mixed with some business with his German jewel dealers. This little junket also provided more confusion for the smugglers regarding exactly what we were up to, if anything.

I met Yosif for a long lunch at the Maaschanz restaurant located right on the Main River. He wore the same all-black attire—slacks, turtleneck shirt, coat, and dress shoes—his trademark now. We gave each other a big hug. Yosif filled me in on what had happened back in Afghanistan and Peshawar.

"Well, Abdul, my dear friend, everything is set. The remaining part of the equipment you ordered has safely reached Shah's cousin's farm, with no problems whatsoever. The wireless communications equipment and mine detector were easily disassembled for ease of concealment through all the border checks."

"Fantastic. Everything is falling in place. Any word around Peshawar about our hoodlum friends?"

"Only that they're still mystified about the location of the jewels and what plans we might have to collect them. They're probably waiting to see when we all get together again in Peshawar to head out towards the border. You and your men need to be as inconspicuous as possible the day before you go over into Afghanistan."

Yosif and I stayed several days, relaxing at a private villa, loaned to him by one of his clients. We needed to wait for the arrival of the new moon, before flying back to Pakistan. The three bedroom, handsomely-furnished villa was snuggled amongst sprawling, rolling hills of grape vineyards along the Main River, just south of the town of Wicker. The locals considered the small, quaint town the gateway to the Rheingau wine region, located about twenty kilometers west.

After we went over the final, small details of the mission, we talked very little about it in the following few days. We simply spoke of the old times when Afghanistan was a wonderful country to live in and raise a family.

We walked down the long rows of healthy grapevines and reminisced about the good life Kabul once offered, before the communists started their behind-the-scenes influence to corrupt the minds of our youths.

"Abdul, our families and friends knew we had to change over from a monarchy towards a more democratic form of government. But the United States chose not to support Afghanistan with financial aid and education when we asked them in the fifties. They chose to keep their alliance with Pakistan. We had nowhere to turn. The Soviet Union gladly offered to help us, with open arms."

Yosif grabbed a handful of ripe Riesling grapes left dangling on a vine from the harvest and popped several into his mouth.

"You're right. Pakistan got in the way of us receiving help from the United States. They used their advantageous geographical position of being an effective military buffer between India and Russia. They hold the Darwian Strip—the gateway to the Arabian Sea and the Gulf. This land was taken from us when Pakistan became a country, and now they have ended up sitting pretty.

"Pakistan is helping us now, only because if the Russians win, they'll fall prey to the Soviets' military machine. How sweet of them. The Russians want access to the sea, no matter who they have to take out.

"One of these days, maybe the tables will turn. Right now Pakistan wants to control us. But, I wouldn't worry about it. The Pashtuns have always kept Afghanistan free."

"Always," said Yosif.

The heat from the sun's rays beat down on bare earth beneath our feet. Trapped within the topsoil all day long, it now began to slowly rise with the cool of the evening coming on. The smell of damp, fertile soil rose to greet my nostrils, with every step I took. The lazy, constant flow of the Main River had nurtured these hills for hundreds of years.

I changed the subject. "Afghanistan was making a change for the better until the Communists took over the government. Prime Minister Daoud of the Royal Family tried to make some democratic social changes—especially emancipation rights for women, by allowing them equal access to the universities and the lifting of the veil."

"Yes, indeed," Yosif said and popped a few more grapes into his mouth. "But some of the more conservative religious leaders did not agree with removing veils from our women.

"Daoud was right when he pointed out that the Koran doesn't say anything about the necessity of women veiling themselves." I squatted down to grab a handful of the rich soil.

"Exactly, and unfortunately, for Afghanistan, the Russians had their claws deep into Daoud with a hidden agenda." Yosif spit out the grape seeds. "Daoud should have ferreted out their true imperialist intentions a lot earlier than they did. Because, by the time he tried to do something, the Communists had their way with our more educated youth, who we gladly sent over to Russia to receive a better education in their government-controlled universities."

"To be brainwashed is more appropriate," I said. "It turned out they recruited a good majority of our graduates to become either members of the Communist Party or spies for the KGB. One of those Russian college graduates who killed my brother in front of my family home, the day after the Soviet troops invaded the capital, had been an old neighbor of ours in Kabul back in the early seventies. Hell, I went to school with him. I want revenge on him." I threw the soil in my hands, down hard to the ground.

"Relax, Abdul. The traitorous murderers will be dead soon, if they're not already. Relax. It's beautiful here in these German hills."

"Yes, yes. It is beautiful here." I dug the front toes of my shoes into the dark brown soil. "I'm sorry. I just can't believe what our countrymen are doing to each other."

"Like you said, they've been brainwashed, My Dear Friend. They will pay the ultimate price in the end. Either by another brother's hand, or Allah in his own special way. Be patient." Yosif patted me gently on my back. "Say, why don't we take a drive up into Wicker this evening and have dinner at a local winery?"

"Sounds good. You're right, I should relax while we're here. satisfaction will come when we retrieve the jewels and get the rest of my family out of Kabul." I gave Yosif a firm slap on the back.

"That's the spirit! I'll buy dinner. The restaurant prepares an excellent roasted lamb dish that rivals our own back home."

"You're on." I gave Yosif a big smile.

I finally relaxed after awhile and, temporarily forgot about our nation's predicament. As it turned out, I definitely needed to.

CHAPTER 8

Back into Afghanistan

I flew back to Pakistan only three days before a new moon. I left several days before Yosif, because I needed to rendezvous with Shah and Farid to trek back into Afghanistan.

Paranoid from my abduction on the flight out of Karachi in June, I felt both relieved and elated when I easily passed through customs during the middle of the night at Karachi International—courtesy of Farid's influence.

Early the next morning I caught the domestic flight to Peshawar. Shah had a relative waiting for me at the air terminal to give me a ride into the city. Of cardinal importance to the success of our mission was secrecy. The jewel smugglers posted lookouts at the airport keeping an eye out for suspicious people or enemies of their organization. So, to hide my identity on the return to Peshawar, I stepped off the plane donning the more traditional Pakistani dress, with the shawl from my turban draped over my face.

Dropped off at Sher's house by a taxi, I called Shah to tell him my trip back went smoothly. He told me he and Farid would pick me up early the next morning to drive us to the Free Zone for the trek back into Afghanistan. He said to prepare myself for a full two day's trip to his cousin's farm in the village of Noar-A-Amir.

Shah assured me that Farid had finally sold the Land Rover to a client. Farid's younger brother, Wali, would drive us in his modest, older Toyota pickup with an extended cab. Perfect.

They picked me up at sunrise at the same place as last time—two streets down from the photo studio. Fortunately, our hookup went down without a public spectacle. We didn't say much during our drive to the Free Zone. Wali dropped us off at the border without anyone taking special notice.

When we finally walked over the border and headed into the first ravine, we lightened up a little. I especially needed to—during the ride to the border, the tension had tightened my shoulder and neck muscles to the point of causing a nagging headache. We sat down to eat, and chat a little.

"Well, Farid, Shah, how did things go during my stay overseas? Any problems?"

Farid answered. "Everything went fine for us. As Yosif told you, the three machine guns and equipment were transported piece-by-piece to Khier Hammad's farm."

"Yes." Shah chimed in. "And, we have a surprise for you. Farid purchased a grenade launcher from one of his customers for a very good price—two hundred dollars. It's there at the farm."

"Fantastic," I said, then hesitated. "Was anyone suspicious about the transaction?"

"None whatsoever," Farid said.

"Okay. Hopefully we won't have to use it, but you never know."

"Yes, exactly," Farid agreed. "While you were gone, though, the smugglers asked a lot of questions about your whereabouts—when you would be back, and so forth. As far as we can tell, the gangsters are still in the dark about our plans for the jewels."

"That's good for now, gentlemen. But in the next few days they'll figure out that you both are missing, and with Yosif coming back into town tomorrow, suspicion will be raised. They'll probably check out the airport ticket records and discover I'm also back in the area. Those goons will figure out something is up. It's very important that we get in and out of Afghanistan in five days time, if at all possible."

Shah interjected. "That will depend upon whether or not you can lead us to the jewels' exact location at the fort. They could have shifted position since the heavy monsoon rains—several feet by now—or possibly be buried deeper with all the new mud that slid down from the surrounding hills."

"I know, I know. Don't worry, I'll direct us to the jewels. They will be there. Have faith."

They're sticking with me. Their trust and lives are in my hands. My God, this whole effort for these jewels could get us killed.

"We do. That's why we are here with you," Farid said.

The three of them smiled, nodding in agreement.

The warm weather felt good on my face. Quite a difference compared to the last time Shah and I went through the pass in the ice cold rain. This time we took a less traveled route, but at the same elevation as before.

I stopped for a minute, bent down and dug out a small hole in the ground easily with my knife.

"There shouldn't be any problem digging around the grounds at the fort when we get there," I said.

*   *   *

Several hours later my out of shape body ached from the hike.

Damn, Abdul. So hard to get in shape, yet so easy to lose it after lying around for several months.

About fifteen kilometers into our trek through two passes as planned, a friend of Farid's named Zabi, a former commercial airline pilot out of Kabul, picked us up in his pickup truck. Farid had some personal business to attend to with him. We planned to stay for just an hour or two to rest and visit with Zabi's wife and three children.

A very bumpy thirty-minute ride got us to Zabi's place, located in the hills twenty kilometers from Noar-A-Amir.

We drove up to the Zabi's farm, and I thought the house looked as if it belonged to an established trader of livestock or grain. Around the hills, I could make out a few less formidable, older farms spread a kilometer or more apart. Zabi's farm had a solid four-foot adobe wall that entirely surrounded the property thirty feet away from the house. The wall kept in sheep, goats, chickens, and the like.

In reality, the farm was only one of the many safe houses servicing Farid's underground railroad to smuggle Afghans out of the country.

The house belonged to Zabi's family and Farid paid them decent money to use their home as a front. Other sheep and goat herders, including traders in the area, would at times keep some of their animals on the property to give the Afghan and Soviet armies the illusion that Zabi was a successful trader.

Zabi needed the money. He had left his job as a pilot four years ago, when the Afghan Communist regime starting giving preference to commercial pilots who joined the communist party or sympathized with their cause. Zabi quietly quit and returned to his family and properties along the border.

The house looked fairly new, about twenty years old, and the plastered adobe on the outside appeared to be recently re-done. We walked into their home which housed four large separate rooms—two of them good-sized bedrooms. From the furnishings, I could tell Zabi had made an upper middle-class income as a commercial pilot. Beautiful Afghan rugs graced the cement floors, and ornamental brass and copper pots adorned the windowsills and several wooden tables. The living room was spacious, and the kitchen had a movable metal awning roof that rolled back on wooden tracks, exposing a mosquito netting top for the hot summer months. A cool breeze swept through the front door and out through the rear bedroom windows and the screened-in kitchen.

Zabi cheerfully greeted us. "Welcome to our abode. Are you sure you won't spend the night? We have sleeping rolls stowed away in the back for those times when Farid's people bring the families through and they need to put them up for a day or two for safekeeping."

"No, thank you, but thanks for the invitation," Farid replied. "We're on a tight schedule. Shah promised his cousins we would arrive sometime early tomorrow evening. We need to get as far as possible this evening—at least halfway there. Again, thanks, though."

Zabi didn't know about the nature of our true business. Farid instructed his people, who came through days earlier, to inform Zabi that our trip regarded resistance matters. The less people to know about the jewels, the better for everyone's sake.

Zabi's wife, Miriam, came out with some freshly-baked Naan bread with honey, pieces of left-over roasted chicken, and hot tea. She looked just a few years younger than her husband, who I guessed to be about ten years older than Farid—maybe thirty-five.

She had big brown eyes and jet black hair down to her waist. Miriam spoke Pashtu and Farci—her diction in Farci perfect. Though she dressed in the traditional clothing for women in this area, she wore no veil. Most women in the country did not. Farid had told us she was one of the few women who attended the University of Kabul, in the seventies. Zabi met her there.

"Welcome to our home," Miriam said happily. "If you need anything, please feel free to ask me. You look like you're a little tired. Please stretch out and relax. Farid, I've been waiting to thank you for the gift of glazed pottery ware your men brought to us last week. It's very handsome and well made. Thank you!"

"Yes, Farid, many thanks," Zabi added. "Miriam loves the dinnerware. She's used the set almost every night since it came."

"I figured with all the people that stop by here, you might need extra. Both of you have been such gracious hosts to my men and the families they bring through. I often hear from former clients. They write to me from England, Germany, and the United States, to say thanks again for smuggling them out. Many of the letters ask about you. They mention the tremendous hospitality your family showed them during their stay."

"That's kind. Miriam is quite the host." Zabi smiled at his lovely bride.

But then, he changed the subject, "Abdul, how did your flight into Karachi International turn out? Did you pass through customs without any problems?"

"Yes, yes, thanks to Farid. When I first got off the plane I was nervous. I didn't know what to expect, because of my ordeal with customs when I flew out of the Karachi terminal on my way to Frankfurt, in May."

Farid, who sat next to me on the floor, put his hand on my shoulder and interrupted. "Yes, that was very unfortunate. I didn't get a chance to arrange things before Abdul left. We really didn't think they would strip search him when he left the country. They must have been told there was something important on him, which there wasn't."

The sorry bastards hoped I had the jewels on me. That customs official had to have been on the gangster's payroll.

"Anyway, Zabi," I continued, "as soon as I exited the airplane's door onto the top of the portable stairway, a swarm of mosquitoes, I mean hundreds of them, engulfed me. Everyone left the plane with their arms flailing about, to protect their faces from the relentless attack. It was one-thirty in the morning and the portable flood lights really attracted them. They covered every passenger. We ran like madmen to the terminal. The armed guards on the runway were prepared though—the men had mosquito netting over them. I've never seen it so bad in my life."

"I know, I know. I've seen it like that once or twice before, when I flew the international flights. With the huge amount of rain this year it's really bad, especially with Karachi having no sewers. They get huge there, too."

"Listen, you don't have to tell me," I said, and made a sour face. Zabi's three children sitting at the door of the bedroom watching and listening, giggled with their hands over their mouths.

"You think insect infestation in Karachi is bad, you should see some places in India," Farid said. "Last year, about this time, during a short business trip to Old Delhi, I went up to a fruit-stand vendor and asked him where his watermelon was. He said 'right there' pointing off to the side of him. I looked over and couldn't see a watermelon anywhere, until he brushed his hand over a spot that was all black. The black area disappeared, when several hundred flies flew away, revealing a ripe, cut piece of watermelon."

"Sounds delicious!" Shah joked, licking his lips. Miriam and the children laughed out loud in delight.

"Anyway, getting back to customs, everything went perfect. Although, like I said, I was a little nervous. I carried quite a bit of American money on me, plus some instructional paperwork on the weapons we use for the resistance effort and such. But, not to worry, Farid had arranged for everything. You would think I was a Pakistani official." I reached over and slapped Farid on the back.

"Tell them how you were treated," Farid said, looking proud.

"A senior customs officer, a very tall man for a Pakistani, came up to me while I was standing in line and asked if I was Abdul Barkzi. I told him yes, and he asked me to follow him to his office. Once inside, he offered me a cup of tea, then asked for my tickets, passport, and visa. I gave them to him, and he told me to wait there, that he would be right back. Ten minutes later he returned and had an assistant carry my bags. The senior officer gave me my paperwork all stamped and in order. Then they politely escorted me through several checkpoints and out the front door of the terminal to a waiting, hired car.

"As I got inside the car, he leaned over and said with a smile, 'Your connecting plane to Peshawar leaves this morning at nine forty-five. The driver will take you to a comfortable hotel right down the road, so you can catch a few hours sleep before your flight. This hospitality is all compliments of your new friend in Peshawar—Farid.' The customs officers both got a chuckle from my surprised look of relief."

"That's great," said Zabi. "Farid really knows his business, yes?"

Farid cut in. "What you didn't know, Abdul, is that the customs official is of Pashtun descent, and has family living all along the Free Zone. Though he works for the Pakistan government, he's one of us."

"Without a doubt," I said.

After we finished our meal, Shah and I lay our heads

down on some soft, down-filled pillows for a half-hour rest, while Farid went off with Zabi to discuss their personal business. As we left, we told Zabi that we would spend the night, on our way back to Pakistan.

Our next trek to Noar-A-Amir would take us into the night, before we'd reached beyond the halfway point.

No sweat, I felt like a new man after our meal and rest at Zabi's farm.

All three of us hiked aggressively, mentally primed for the mission ahead. We made great time in the rough, roller-coaster terrain.

Two hours after sunset, the eve of a new moon, the sky and barren landscape took on a new life. The night sky glowed from the infinite number of stars that shone radiantly bright, so clear and intense that many resembled distant planets. What a stark difference to what I had viewed in the mountains of upstate New York a month ago. The Milky Way filled the northwest sky. It looked rather like a large swirl of cotton candy enticing you to reach out and take a piece with your hand.

The rains of monsoon season had washed all dust from the land. The high mountain cliffs glittered as large crystals in this pristine night, their sheared sides mirrored the sky above. The terrain and sky turned into a kaleidoscope of starry delights known for centuries only to these Pashtuns.

About eleven o'clock, we heard the labored sound of a large aircraft approaching us from the southwest.

"It a C-17 coming in for a drop," said Shah. "They might be making a drop to the valley just below us. There are several Mujahidin storage caves right around here."

Air America, the CIA's air operations effort leftover from the Vietnam theater, were back in action in Afghanistan.

Every new moon, C-17s flew in for several nights at predesignated Mujahidin-controlled valleys to make drops of medical supplies, clothing, food, and munitions. As soon as the palettes hit the ground, our people loaded their pack mules and quickly headed back into the mountains to well-concealed caves undetectable to Soviet aircraft.

Retired Air Force pilots manned these older air cargo planes. They took off from airfields in Turkey, flew in from the south over the Arabian Sea into Pakistan and, once in southern Afghanistan, they hugged the ground to avoid radar detection as they flew their way to the Kyber region. Here, in this mountainous region, the veteran pilots and their huge planes were put to the real test.

"It sounds as if the plane is climbing that ridge thirty kilometers direct south from here," Shah said, pointing to a ridge that rose at least thirteen-thousand feet high.

"Those guys have a lot of guts to fly in here under these no-moon conditions and high terrain," I said.

"Without a doubt," said Farid. "I've seen a lot of close calls on my smuggling runs to Kabul and back."

The sound of the plane's engines turned into a roar as it cleared the top of the mountain's crest. Immediately, the big bird's props cut back to descend down towards the valley. I strained to see the C-17, to no avail. A minute later, I barely made out the dark outlines of the large chutes against the starry sky, floating down towards the valley floor.

The engines kicked in again with a high-pitched roar. Several long minutes later, the laborious sound disappeared over the mountain tops to the east. The old-timer and his plane again made their way safely over to Pakistan.

Around one o'clock in the morning, we grew tired from hiking and lay down within the cover of large boulders. The magnificent display of meteors' showers lulled me to sleep.

We awoke six hours later to complete our final leg of the journey. For the entire day, we hiked hard, taking only a few short breaks to rest in the shade of shallow caves and grab a bite to eat to keep up our stamina.

A large, crimson sun was setting low over the high desert valley when we finally walked into the village, quiet, but for the crows of a few stubborn roosters who decried the day's end.

We trudged to the edge of town, to Kheir Hammad's farm. We saw only a few farmers walking along their irrigation canals with shovels, ready to clean out silt that might restrict the flow of the precious water that gave life to their crops.

The village of Noar-A-Amir, to a Westerner, would look like a small, lush, golf course sitting alone, totally isolated on a Wali desert landscape. Almost as if a mirage, that a man dying of thirst, might imagine. From a bird's eye view, each farm resembled well-kept golf fairways of various shades of green, intertwined with each other. Gray-stone fences, tall juniper pines, and full, mature fruit and walnut trees, outlined every property.

Under the thickest groups of trees, farmers' homes nestled in the shade—simple houses, made of traditional brick, stick and mud construction—with hard dirt floors.

The farmers' existence depended upon the brisk-flowing river running alongside the village—given its name after the river itself—the Noar-A-Amir meaning River of Amir.

The river, fed from the melting snows of the Hindu Kush mountains, provided the lifeline of these villagers. Without it, the village would blow away like dust, leaving only gray rocks and boulders to remain—a few armadillos or lizards occasionally taking refuge under them from the sun's harsh rays. But shallow irrigation ditches, dug out by each farmer's family, let the river's water flow into the farms, bringing forth abundant life: a true oasis in this rough, barren land.

We finally came to Kheir Hammad's farmhouse. His son, Ghulam, about my age but taller, sharpened a shovel and farming hoe just outside the front door.

Ghulam looked up, spotted us, and shouted inside the house, "Kheir! Shah and his friends are here!"

Within a few seconds, his father eagerly appeared through the door and waved at us.

"There is the rest of our team," Shah said. He jogged ahead to greet his cousins.

"We made the second day of our adventure without a hitch," Farid smiled.

"Yes, we did. Things are looking good so far. Tomorrow evening promises to be exciting."

"You mean nerve-racking?"

"That too," I replied.

We had a fantastic meal that evening, prepared by one of Kheir's nieces in the village, named Sheila. Kheir's wife had died several years back from a stroke, so Sheila helped the two men practically on a daily basis.

Sheila came over early in the morning, especially for our visit, to prepare a special dinner for us. She cooked *Pilau Quabli*, a special casserole made with local rice, raisins, diced carrots, almonds, and pistachios. With the dish, she also served a bowl of curried chicken and rice, several plates of cooked vegetables, and Naan bread.

Kheir had aged well beyond a man of forty-eight years, with a long, snow-white beard and deeply-recessed wrinkles that enveloped his dark eyes filled with wisdom. He had seen a lot in his lifetime, but seemed to have plenty of life and strength in him, still.

"We're not used to having such a grand meal, except for our weekly family gatherings after mosque and other local celebrations here in the village," stated Kheir. "Of course, Sheila honors special guests like you in our home. We hope everything was to your satisfaction. She slaved over the hearth since sunrise to prepare this fine meal for us. Sheila is like a daughter to me, and a dear sister to Ghulam. Her husband is understanding. We help each other out. Where one lacks, the other makes up."

"This meal was a treat, very delicious and satisfying," Shah said thankfully. He turned to Farid and me. "Gentlemen, to your liking?"

Before Farid could give a charming, well drawn-out thanks, I spoke up, "As Farid and I mentioned to each other over this wonderful dinner, we haven't had a country-cooked meal like this in a long time—years, in fact. We feel completely at home, just like the good old days, back as young men in a free Afghanistan."

I turned to Sheila standing in the doorway of the kitchen to embellish on the compliment. "Thank you very much for everything. *The Pilau Qablin* was especially delicious—just like my mother used to cook it."

Sheila blushed and took a quick, graceful bow, then-turned around, to return to her kitchen work.

"She's bashful when she first meets strangers," stated Ghulam.

After dinner, we chatted about how Farid planned to have some of his best men smuggle my sister, sister-in-law, and their children out of Kabul. The group would rendezvous with us a day after we returned back to Zabi's safe house.

An hour later, totally beat from the long trek, the three

of us retired for the evening.

The next morning it took several hours to sketch out detailed maps of the area around the fort. We discussed who would be stationed where, how to approach with the least risk of mines, and how Kheir and Ghulam would dig the ground near the boulder, for the buried jewels.

The rest of the day we accustomed ourselves to the wireless communications headsets. Good thing we did, because we discovered damage from shipping in one of the headsets. Fortunately, Mike and Storm Mor had thrown in an extra headset for good measure.

At six thirty, after the sunset, the five of us took off for the fort, still eighteen kilometers away by foot. We moved as fast as possible, to ensure having the time needed to secure our lookout posts for the evening. Kheir and Ghulam's hiking skills were right up to speed with ours.

Though Kheir had spent most of his time around the farm since his wife's passing, his occasional participation in Mujahidin raids had apparently kept him in good shape.

Ghulam, on the other hand, had the demanding job of shepherding their sheep throughout the year, in addition to the final herding of them to market. He also participated in the Mujahidin raids with his father. To say the least, he could run circles around all of us.

They both knew the lay of the land towards the fort by rote, including the short cuts and easiest terrain to cross over. We moved much faster than the night before. Kheir kept *Naswar* under his tongue—a stronger Pashtun version of American snuff, made of ground tobacco and hot spices—to provide him the extra stimuli he needed to hike at our quick pace. His mouth constantly fell agape to help cool the hot sensation that built up around his tongue, which gave him a rather idiotic look.

Just after ten, we arrived above the foothills overlooking the fort. The toughest part of the expedition lay ahead of us. We had devised a fairly simple plan.

Two sloping hills overlooked the jewels' hiding place, located about five feet away from the boulder I had fought behind.

Our approach called for taking two different positions on the hills to observe and direct the digging. The selected sites were elevated one hundred feet higher than the boulder below. The slope on the east side was 250 yards away from the site, with the one to the west, 150 yards way—much closer to the boulder, as well as the fort's corner guard tower, only sixty yards further down.

Shah assigned Ghulam and his father to do the digging, and refused to allow me to go down. That night, over dinner when I talked him into the campaign, he clearly stated that I had put my life in peril too many times. He said he felt responsible for talking me into going on the last raid.

Ghulam and his father approached the boulder from the western position. Farid stayed behind on the west slope to observe through his night glasses. From his vantage point he would communicate to me, via the headset, the progress of Kheir and his son and report any sentry movements along the fort walls.

I directed the moves from the eastern slope, farthest away, as I looked through the night-vision glasses and communicated through the headsets to Kheir and Farid. Shah knelt at my side.

The bright stars provided enough illumination for everyone to see a slight shadow of themselves.

As father and son proceeded down the slope, except for

the green tint, their movements through the night glasses reminded me of the first televised pictures of the Apollo astronauts walking around the moon. The scene looked like a slow motion sequence with ghosting trails of their motions following behind them.

As they went farther down the hill, I gave Kheir, who wore the third headset, step-by-step directions to the exact location.

It took close to two hours for them to slowly inch towards the boulder from Farid's position on the west slope. Kheir, with the help of the night glasses, led with the mine detector, while Ghulam hung on to the back of his shirt. When Kheir found a land mine, Ghulam gathered small rocks, piled them together, and then, placed them just to the right of the concealed mine. Therefore, on their return trip, they could quickly follow the piles of rocks back to safety. I heard them quietly bickering from time to time about where to place the stones. Other than that, all was dead silent.

They finally reached the boulder, and started to dig around the area where I had buried the jewel sack. After they had dug for close to an hour, tempers started to flare. Farid's, Kheir's and my own voice raised almost to a point of shouting into the headsets.

"The jewels are not here. We've dug all around the place you say they are, and they're not here!" Kheir said.

"Of course they are! They must have shifted directly downhill during the heavy rains. You have been digging to the left and right of the spot. Listen to what I'm telling you. You need to dig down farther, straight down."

"Are you sure? Could they be higher up than you thought?" Farid said.

"Of course, I'm sure!"

After several minutes of argument, I finally blew my cool with the constant bickering.

"Damn it, this is no good. There are too many people giving instructions. I'm the only one who should be giving the orders. It's over. The fort's searchlight may come on soon. We'll have to try again tomorrow night. We're out of here. Now!"

On the way back to the village, no one spoke a word. When we got back to Kheir's home, it was close to four o'clock in the morning. We lay down to sleep. Morning sunrise prayer would come early.

I dozed off and on, all night. The jewels' resting place haunted my mind.

After morning prayer, all five of us sat down for a light meal and to discuss our predicament. I couldn't eat.

The meeting got off to a bad start. Everyone argued. We placed blame on each other as to who screwed up. Within minutes, the discussion turned into a shouting match. The house dog and goat scurried out the door, their tails quivering between their legs.

"Listen," I said. "If you had followed my original plan, we would be on our way back with the jewels! Tonight, we go in and I'll be the only one who gives directions on where to dig. I'm the one who knows where the jewels are—no one else."

"We dug where you told us to last night," Ghulam said.

"Yes, at first. When they weren't there, I figured the jewels had moved almost straight down, because of the mud slides, and I told you to dig straight down. But, you kept digging to the left and right of the original resting place. Again, you must dig straight down. That's where they are."

"Listen, Abdul, how do you know the stones haven't already been found by someone?" said Shah.

"Because the word would have been out by now. Even if a local villager had found them, he would have to find a buyer. Yosif, or one of his contacts, would have heard about it already."

Everyone went silent for a moment.

"Listen, gentlemen, we will find the jewels if you follow my lead. But it is very important that we find them tonight. The trail is getting hot on us. We must not fail, or we'll go home empty-handed. All of our time and work will be for nothing. We must succeed!"

"O.K., O.K. we are with you," Farid said.

The others nodded in firm agreement.

Shah stood up. "Let's get some rest. Try to catch three or four hours sleep, if possible. After we retrieve the jewels tonight, we are going to have a long trip to get back over the border. Right, Abdul?"

"Absolutely," I said softly, with a halfhearted smile.

But, as it turned out, I couldn't sleep. I tossed and turned, constantly thinking about the satchel of gems.

Our backs were to the wall with time running out. The longer we stayed around, the more we exposed ourselves to curious nomadic traders who could be possible informants for the bastards in Peshawar.

About one o'clock in the afternoon, I heard Sheila's cries of despair.

"Kheir, Ghulam, wake up!" she screamed. "Our dear neighbor Karim has been killed in a shovel fight with the eldest son of the Jamal family." Her face streamed with tears. She fell to her knees. Splatters of blood stained the bottom of her dress.

"The stupid feud over last week's standoff over the water canal rights has taken your beloved friend's life!"

"What are you saying Sheila? I can't believe my ears," Kheir shouted. "Who slayed the old man—the Jamals'?"

"Yes, yes. Karim tried to intervene between his son and two cousins and Jamal's three sons, who were dueling with their shovels over the rationing rights for the day. It started out not so bad, with only Karim's son, Hamid, and Jamal's son, Shafi, going at it. Almost as if they were joking around, play fighting."

"Play fighting? Joking around?"

"Yes. Then Hamid winged Shafi's arm, and all six of them went at it in anger. Karim saw what was happening and stepped in the middle of the fight between Hamid and Shafi, trying to stop it. Shafi hit Karim square over the head with the edge of the shovel. He dropped to the ground, his head split wide open. I cradled his head in my lap, trying to wake him up. But it didn't do any good. My God, look at me, I'm covered in his blood!"

"He deliberately killed the old man?" Ghulam said.

"It could have been an accident, I can't be sure. It looked like Shafi didn't see Karim as he stepped in between them. Shafi was blinded by rage. Does it really matter? Karim is dead. What happens now?"

"Where are both families?" Kheir shouted.

"The townspeople separated the two families and are keeping them under watch at the mosque. Karim's body is in his house. Hamid is demanding an immediate gun duel with Shafi, or threatens otherwise, to bring in the PDPA Communist police. Kheir, what are we to do? Please, Kheir, Ghulam, you must go see the elders."

"Ghulam, come. Shah, keep your friends here. We'll be

back as soon as we can."

Kheir packed an old Colt 45 under his shirt, and they headed out the door.

"There's going to be trouble," said Shah. "Kheir knew Karim since childhood, and Hamid is like a brother to Ghulam."

Damn it! This is not what we need. We have to find the jewels tonight—it's our last chance.

Farid, Shah, and I stared at each other in disbelief. Our own countrymen's show of arrogant machismo had put our mission in further jeopardy.

Except for wars, since my childhood, shovel fighting had accounted for most of the violent deaths in my world. They were usually prompted when family clans argued over what days their family had access to the main water canal. And, if one called another a liar, all hell would break loose.

We laid low for nearly two hours, waiting for the news on the clan quarrel, then Kheir and Ghulam showed up with their long faces.

Kheir gave out a long sigh and then spoke. "Before the elders could rule, Hamid broke loose of the men holding him and ran off shouting he would have his due revenge. In the confusion, Shafi took off after him, still in a rage. We followed them, but by the time we arrived, it was too late."

"Too late?" cried Shah.

"Yes. This time the stroke of revenge ended with Hamid slaying Shafi. A bloody mess. Shafi's head was nearly severed off by Hamid's knife. Hamid must have had it concealed on him all the while."

"He had the right," Shah said.

"The elders have gone to consider the situation. Hamid will be under house arrest at an elders farmhouse until

Friday, after the Mosque, when the council's vote will have decided upon his fate. We are hoping no one will get the authorities involved. Until tonight, keep out of sight in the back room."

With his chin lowered, and mumbling to himself, Khier slowly walked across the room to his bedroom.

"Let's try to get a few more hours of sleep," said Ghulam. "We'll leave around seven-thirty this evening, less than three hours from now. Let my father and I get some rest, please."

We all lay down on the floor mats to try to sleep.

I slept restlessly, dozing off only once. Shah and Farid tossed and turned the entire time. As the sun started to set in the distant valley, we rose to gear up for the hike. No one had much to say.

The trek to the fort seemed to take a lot less time than before. When we got to the fort and positioned ourselves at the overlook areas, Kheir and his son took off for the boulder. Their rock pile markings from the night before had stayed in tack and led them straight to the designated spot. In less than five minutes, they shoveled dirt.

This time only my voice and Kheir's spoke on the headsets. I told him where to dig and he'd respond "O.K." After they dug the first six holes without any luck, I started to panic. I wiped the dripping sweat from my brow and neck.

Shah gently patted me on my back, whispering, "It's all right. You will find them. Be patient, they are there. Just a little further down, that's all—have faith."

Even Farid remarked over the headset, "Don't worry, they're down there, you'll see. The jewels will soon be ours."

By the seventh attempt, Kheir's tone had changed. He sounded rather hesitant, anxious.

Then, suddenly, hope returned to Kheir's voice. "Just a minute, Abdul, hold on for a few minutes. Ghulam and I will dig down further using our hands."

Kheir took off his headset, laid it on the ground, and knelt down next to his son. They dug quickly.

Dead silence hovered over the three of us watching from above.

Finally, Kheir stood up. His silhouette revealed him holding a bag high up in the air, shaking it.

Shah and I embraced in jubilation. We could feel each others' laughs and cries. I held back my urge, fearing it would give away our presence to the sleeping sentries. I looked over towards the western slope and watch Farid through the night goggles, gleefully dancing around in circles.

Shah and I ran over to Farid and waited, as Kheir and Ghulam cautiously walked back.

As soon as they returned to the western slope, I took a fast look into the bag.

"It looks like they're all here," I whispered in delight.

We packed up our equipment and I placed the satchel of precious stones firmly over my shoulder. Then we ran up the hill as if a pack of jackals were behind us.

Adrenaline overwhelmed me, similar to the morning of the raid when I had run towards the hills—except this time, no chopper missiles exploded behind me. Still, the thought of the fort's high beam searchlight striking out to expose our retreat frightened me to where my legs ached and felt unbearably heavy. They ached to the point where I worried I would fall. I pushed myself to run, thinking, *Run...Abdul. Move your legs, for God's sake, Run!*

We finally made it over into the next gully and stopped, all of us wheezing. We grabbed our breaths, and said our quick farewells.

"Thank you very much for everything Kheir and Ghulam," I said. "I'm very sorry for the extent of our arguing the last twenty-four hours, but my nerves were almost shot. I didn't want this mission to be a bust for us."

"No need to apologize. All of us were pretty much on edge," Kheir replied. "You were right, though. They were straight down. The mud slides must have been pretty bad on those slopes this year."

Shah smiled at his cousins and said, "Kheir, Ghulam, I'll have your share delivered to you in the next several weeks after everything calms down."

Kheir responded, "I know you will. Thank you for giving us the opportunity to make this kind of money. It's more money than my son and I have made in five years."

"Yes, yes, thank you very much," said Ghulam.

We said our final good-byes, and father and son took off with most of the weapons and equipment strapped around them. They would hide them between here and their village for future resistance use.

The three of us headed out for Zabi's house. I checked my watch. Twelve o'clock midnight.

We would try to hike for three more hours, and then get several hours of sleep. The stars glistened more beautiful than ever. The sky and landscape had their jewels. We had ours.

Zabi and Miriam greeted us as we walked up to the front gate of the compound.

"Welcome back, gentlemen! We have some people inside the house who are anxious to see you," said Zabi happily.

I ran in the front door, with Shah and Farid right behind me. My sister, Nafisa, and my sister-in-law, Hanifa—along with a host of children: four boys and seven girls—had all lined up in the front room. Each of them held a bouquet of wild flowers. As we walked in, they shouted, "Abdul and friends, thank you for giving us our freedom. May Allah bless you!"

I hugged my sister with joy.

"Thank God you made it out of Kabul alive," I said. "How are you?"

"I'm doing O.K. considering what the whole family has gone through the past three years."

I hadn't seen Nafisa in over seven years, and apparently, her last few years had taken their toll. At twenty-seven—only two years older than I—her hair had turned prematurely gray. Before I had left for the states to attend college, everyone thought of her as one of the most beautiful young ladies, a catch for the well-educated Afghan man who ended up marrying her. Then, after the Soviet takeover, her husband fled from home to escape prison or execution.

He now worked with underground resistance efforts just outside Kabul. Nafisa told me that she heard from him every month or so, through a messenger. The enormous pressure had aged her well beyond her years.

Hanifa, the same age as Nafisa, showed a few gray hairs as well, but the wrinkles and dark circles under her eyes told an even clearer story of her stress and misery in Kabul. During the first few days of the Soviet invasion, the communists had taken her husband from their home and shot him, just as they did my brother.

All fifteen children—four boys and eleven girls—were between the ages of five and twelve. Six of the children belonged to Nafisa and Hanifa. The two women cared for the remaining nine—distant cousins, either orphaned or whose parents were imprisoned. The Pul-i-Charkhi prison fortress, just outside Kabul, held political prisoners and the KhAD tortured and killed many of the 20,000 inmates.

I listened, as Hanifa and Nafisa told us about getting smuggled out, and how all seventeen walked down the main caravan road, used by refugees. They talked of the slow, arduous trip by foot, mules, and camels, and how the children had sung songs to keep their spirits up.

"They are so happy to be so close to freedom," Nafisa said with a long sigh. "They are looking forward to being able to play outside, to enjoy the freedom of not being questioned by soldiers or killed by a mortar explosion or a stray bullet."

Nafisa's eyes filled with tears.

"I'm so very sorry," I said. "It's been tough for you and all our family."

"Fortunately my husband is still alive, and my children will soon be safe with me when we get to America. But, how are you, Abdul? I heard about your barbaric ordeal through Farid's men. I'm very sorry what they did to you."

"It's O.K. At one point during my capture, I didn't think I would make it. It still takes me an hour or so in the morning to work out the stiffness from the broken bones and damaged nerves. Don't worry about me though, I'll be all right."

"Thank goodness. Hanifa and I want to thank you for paying the money to smuggle us out of Afghanistan. I don't know how you are going to pay for it"

"Don't worry, things have worked out. I have a surprise for you. Come follow me to the back bedroom."

I closed the curtain behind us, grabbed the backpack and opened it wide so she could see inside.

"This has paid for your passage."

Nafisa knees buckled. I grabbed her hand.

"Abdul, where did you get so many precious stones?

There's a fortune in there!"

I quickly recapped the story.

"This is all very amazing. I think you're all crazy—especially you," Nafisa said. "You're tempting fate for the second time. Does Laila know what you're up to?"

I looked away for a moment. "No."

Nafisa shook her finger at me. "Abdul, how could..."

I grabbed her finger. "I didn't want to worry her. Listen, I've now become accustomed to war and its risks. My partners and I will all make it out."

Nafisa stared out the room's window for a moment.

"Yosif, the big man, you knew as a kid. How is he?"

"He's doing great. And, he'll be our protector once we get out of Peshawar tomorrow."

"I don't want to lose another brother. And I know Laila would not approved of this escapade!"

"Why so worried? You're going to be free, yes?"

"Yes, thank you."

"And, soon Laila will have plenty of money, yes?"

"You're nuts."

"Maybe." I chuckled. I gave Nafisa a big hug, and kissed her on her drawn cheek.

We returned back into the main room to visit with the children. They had surrounded Shah and Farid who recounted war stories about the Mujahidin, and told them about the shops and sights they would see in Peshawar. I slipped into the circle to join them. They engulfed me in laughter and questions about life in America. I told them stories for an hour before I had to retire for the evening. It took me another twenty minutes to break away with the help of Hanifa.

Everyone slept soundly that evening. The women and children readied themselves to travel with Farid's men on the main caravan route as before. Right after breakfast, Nafisa and I had told Hanifa about the jewels. I split the jewels up into two smaller pouches—one for each of them to carry concealed under their long, enveloping *chadoris* clothing.

The jewels would be safer with their group for the rest of the trek. No one would suspect them. They would blend in with the throngs of refugees crossing over the border. We would follow them from a comfortable distance to make sure no problems arose.

We made plans for them to stay at another safe house, eight miles outside of Peshawar, for a couple of days. Farid's people needed time to arrange for their passports and tickets before they departed to the states.

Later that evening, I would regain the jewels from them since Shah, Yosif, Farid and I were scheduled for an early morning flight out of Peshawar on the first leg of our escape out of Pakistan.

After they left, the three of us said farewell to Zabi and Miriam. Farid would tell them of our escapade after the jewels were long sold. It was for their safety.

We trekked about a mile behind the main caravan route with my family in sight. About five kilometers from the Free Zone we came across a small Pashtun village. A small boy, maybe five-years-old, came running up to me. He tugged feverishly on my sleeve with his left hand. His right arm had no hand, just a badly scarred stump that still oozed blood and pus.

"Sir, please, can you help my family with food or money? Please, my father has been killed and my mother, sister and I need to take care of my grandfather and us. Please." He started to cry. Tears streamed down his dark, soiled face.

Before I could say a word, a young woman about ten

yards away shouted, "Salem, keep away from those men. Quit begging!"

"It's okay," I shouted back.

More tears ran down Salem's face. "Look what the enemy did to my arm. I can't use it. It hurts."

Shah, Farid, and I already had our hands in our pockets bringing out what dried food we had left.

"Gentleman, I'm very sorry for Salem coming up to you this way," the thin woman said. She was gaunt in the cheeks, and had a fresh scar on the left side of her face, perhaps from a shrapnel wound.

"I have scolded him a hundred times for begging," she said, lifting her long, neatly-combed hair over the scar. "My family was not raised this way."

"What happened to his arm?" I said.

"Two months ago he picked up one of those toy bombs dropped from the sky by the horrible Russian planes. I got to him just as it went off."

I had heard of dreaded plastic toy bombs: motion-activated explosives made up to resemble colorful, little bright red trucks or cars, or yellow butterflies. Soviet aircraft dropped them from the sky, throughout Mujahidin-controlled lines. Hundreds of children had been maimed and killed to help undermine support for the resistance.

"We have some food for you that we don't need," I said. "Please take it. We want you to."

"Yes, yes," said Farid, as he pushed his bag of food and some money towards her. Shah and I gave our rations to the little boy who delightfully grabbed them with one hand.

"We can't," said the mother.

"You must," Shah demanded. "Why haven't the Mujahidin taken you and your family to one of the refugee camps over in Pakistan?"

"They came by once and asked us to go with them, but my grandfather is very sick and wants to die here in his own home. He is very persistent. He doesn't have long to go before he is with Allah—any week now. May Allah please take care of all of you for your kindness."

"Go with God," said Shah.

Both of our parties crossed the border just before sundown without any problems.

Farid's cousin, Wali, picked us up at the scheduled time for our ride back to Peshawar.

"When you guys didn't show up yesterday, I figured you needed another night to find them, yes?"

"We have them," Farid answered.

"Did anybody get hurt?" Wali asked as we got inside the front cab.

"We are just fine," Farid said.

"Can I see the jewels?"

"Maybe when you take us to the airport tomorrow afternoon," I said in delight.

The three of us cracked up. A confused, almost hurt look came to Wali's face. He let go of the steering wheel and threw his hands straight up into the air.

"What's so damn funny?" he asked.

The truck started to veer off the dirt road. Rocks flew in all directions. The truck started to slide uncontrollably towards the side of the steep cliff.

I grabbed the top of Wali's shoulder firmly. "Hands on the wheel, damn it!"

Wali steered out of the skid and slammed on the brakes.

"Are you fucking crazy?" yelled Shah.

Farid started to laugh.

"Farid, shut up. Must you laugh at everything?" Shah yelled, as he slapped Farid on top of his head.

Farid still had a broad smile across his wide face.

Wali just steamed.

"O.K., O.K., I'll let you in on the joke," I said. "We made a bet between the three of us on how long it would take for you to ask to see the jewels. I guessed it would be three questions or less. I won twenty American dollars from each of them."

"Oh, I see," Wali said calmly.

"As far as the precious stones, I'll show them to you tomorrow after I have a chance to go through them. O.K.?"

A smile came back to Wali's face. "Really looking forward to it!"

It was a relief to be dropped off at my cousin's house behind the photography studio. After dinner, I filled Sher in on the details of the past several days. By his awed expression, I could tell he thought Shah was right when he said we were nuts to risk our lives the way we did.

Several hours later, I discretely took a taxi out of Peshawar to the new safehouse for my family. They were overjoyed, especially the children, to be out of Afghanistan. I stayed for a little over an hour—to share the mixed emotions of our homeland's ruin, yet hope for the future. Nafisa handed me the cache of jewels and I went on my way.

I arrived back at Sher's around three-thirty in the morning. My body cried for rest, but my mind spun out of control.

I finally caught an hours sleep before I prepared for my early nine o'clock departure to Lahore.

Though exhausted, I felt satisfied that the jewels were safe with me.

CHAPTER 9

On the Run

*W*ali picked me up that morning in his faithful Toyota truck with Shah already inside. We readied ourselves to head for the terminal to meet Yosif and Farid. Hopefully, they had successfully handled everything, in advance.

Shah and I had decided to dress casually and wore blue jeans and light, short-sleeved shirts. Shah had a leather handbag to carry on. I sported a carry-on bag as well: the backpack that contained the jewels.

"Abdul, I talked to Yosif two hours ago. He said all went well, and that he and Farid would be there ready for the flight." Shah gave me an assured slap on the knee.

"Good," I said.

As promised, along the way to the Peshawar airport, I showed Wali a few of the larger gems.

"Your eyes are as big as melons," Shah said, watching Wali shift his gaze back and forth between the road and the jewels.

Shah said, "Wali, as soon as we sell the gems in Bangkok, I'll take a week's holiday while things cool off. Then, I'll head back to Peshawar to give you your share. O.K.?"

"Fantastic," said Wali.

Though we all smiled, deep down inside me, I knew I'd let out no hearty laugh of triumph until safely underway to India—far from the thugs' influence.

Wali's air conditioning hadn't worked for several years and I sweltered to the point of drenching in sweat. It was like a sauna inside the truck. The radio announcer reported an outside temperature of over 30 degrees centigrade.

We pulled up to a deserted airport terminal, where several Pakistanis sold glasses of ice water along the perimeter of the unloading zone. I tapped Wali on the shoulder. Hang on a minute, while I open my door. I don't know about you guys, but I need some water."

After soaking my handkerchief in the ice cold water, with shaking hands, I cooled my forehead and chest. I desperately needed to make myself appear relaxed when we entered the airport terminal.

Shah gingerly put his arm around me. "Don't worry, Farid and Yosif have taken care of everything. Relax, brother."

"Yes, yes, I know. The heat, the anxiety, along with the over-exhilaration, has left me light headed. Give me a minute to calm down."

I closed my eyes for a moment and tried to talk some sense into myself. I'd handled many situations similar to this before working with the CIA—with the Russians and KhAD agents on my ass.

Fuck those mob bastards—this will be a piece of cake. Walk in like you own the place.

We pulled up to curb side and thanked Wali for all of his help the last week.

Just as Shah closed the cab door, Wali raised his hand and said, "May Allah be with you."

We nodded together in mutual agreement.

Shah and I strode into the front terminal ticket building. Together, as we entered the doorway, I immediately saw Yosif to my right. He casually leaned against one of the empty ticket counters—dressed in his usual all-black attire, minus the turtleneck and coat.

Great. Everything is going to be all right!

Shah nudged me to look over to the left, when Farid walked towards us with tickets and passports in hand.

"Are you ready to go?" He beamed.

"Yes, by all means." I returned the smile.

In jest, Shah tapped me on the back. "Let's go," he said. All three of us moved toward Yosif.

"Glad you made it," Yosif said. "We're ready to go. This way, gentlemen."

Yosif led the way through two, guarded checkpoints. The officials and guards simply smiled and waved us through—out the back exit door towards the runway, where we boarded the plane. I walked on air.

Despite his corrupt use of power and money, Farid's knack for calmly handling airport officials would marvel the finest confidence man or intelligence operator anywhere.

We waited a long half-hour for the rest of the passengers to board. Farid had gotten us seats together, four-across.

As the plane taxied off to the runway, we talked about the unbearable weather and such. When the wheels lifted off the ground, I finally loosened my tense grip on the seat's arm rest.

Praise Allah, we made it!

I slumped back into my seat and felt a smile of relief come over my face.

Within a half an hour of takeoff, I grew tired. I felt relaxed, figuring we had at least a half-day's jump on the Peshawar gang. I dosed off to sleep for the remaining three hours of the flight.

As soon as we landed in Lahore, we hired a taxi to drive us to the Pakistan-India border. When we arrived, there were hundreds of people waiting to cross a narrow stretch of land, 150 meters wide, about half a kilometer long, with fifteen foot, razor-wired fences enclosing both sides.

The wait in line could take a least two to three hours, even before allowing us to cross over, but they had no Farid around. He told us to wait by the main entrance for ten minutes, while he went to make arrangements with his buddies at immigration.

True to his word, he arrived back in ten minutes. "Come on, come on. They want us to go right through. They offered us tea, but I told them we were in an hurry. Let's go!"

We jogged over to the main gate and went right through customs. They asked not a single question. We smiled at the guards, they grinned back. *This is really unbelievable. Is there anyone that Farid doesn't know?*

"Hey, Farid," Yosif said. "Could you get a Catholic friend of mine past the Vatican guards to see the Pope?"

"Sure, why not!" he boasted, with a smirk. "I know quite a few of those young Italian men who dress up in tights and large droopy hats. Just make sure you give me plenty of notice and, then..." Farid clapped his hands together quickly, three times. "No problem!"

"Go, baby, go!," said Yosif, laughing.

Chuckles all around.

As we walked along, hundreds of porters, went back and forth with luggage and packages on their heads. They quickly passed each other in close formation. The ones in blue uniforms were from Pakistan, the ones in orange, Indians. From high above, we probably looked like two different colonies of worker ants, scurrying past each other to get to the other end, wanting to quickly deposit their catch in the nest.

We didn't require porters since we carried only a bag each. The extra backpack I carried weighed at least fifteen pounds, but it didn't bother me. It was a true labor of love, indeed.

We had a quick tea break with the pleasant Indian Sikh officials whom Farid knew. We all laughed about the uneasy relations our countries had experienced with Pakistan.

The Pakistanis had been their adversaries since 1947

when the new Indian Congress split India into two countries. Hindus were forced north, and Muslims south, due to the insistence of the country's spiritual leader, Mahatma Gandhi—who died by the hand of one of his own, a disgruntled Hindu—who disagreed with his tolerance of Indian Muslims.

The officials and guards loved Farid's capitalistic approach to doing business.

We took a taxi from the border, straight to the airport in Amritsar. To our shock, the ticketing clerk told us the airlines postponed our booked flight to Delhi until the next day. A glitch we didn't need right now.

Farid came up with a solution. "Not to worry. A train to Delhi leaves within the hour. Let's hail a taxi right now. We don't have a minute to lose."

Between the unexpected canceled flight and the wild taxi ride, my few hours of feeling somewhat relaxed disappeared and, once again, I turned into an emotional wreck. We had to get to Old Delhi by the evening—at the latest.

Once we got to the train station, it took Farid little time to find some ticket scalpers with four tickets for a fat price—twice the fare. We paid it. Yosif phoned Stella in Amritsar and apologized for our situation. She called ahead to tell our Delhi ticket connection of our late arrival.

We boarded the train just as the last of the porters climbed on.

The train ride to Amritsar turned into quite a humbling experience, especially considering what we had paid for the first-class tickets.

The old train we boarded reminded me of the vintage Orient Express trains in the old spy movies—except this Indian train was in desperate need of repair and refinishing.

The seats in our first class car sat four per stall, two-and-two across from each other. The paneling and the back of the seats of the car were dark, mahogany wood. Thin, worn-out padded leather cushions on each seat provided little comfort. A small table swung down between us so we could spread out our tea and newspapers.

It seemed the only advantages of first class were the extra seats left vacant by the no-shows. We had the car almost to ourselves. At least we had room to move about on the long, eight-hour ride to the capital, because the stagnant heat inside the car soon overwhelmed us. As soon as the train left the station, we pulled the dust-caked screen windows wide open to let more air through.

Opening the screens had its price. Within fifteen minutes, the dust from the outside fields had penetrated us. It stuck to our nostrils, ears, clothing, everything. Within twenty minutes, we had to move to other seats because each of us sat in small pools of mud created from our perspiration having mixed with the dust.

Yosif closed his eyes to either sleep or meditate. Shah, Farid, and I turned our conversation towards our destination, Delhi. This helped to keep my mind off the dust.

Shah had traveled only through Afghanistan and Pakistan. In past chats, he had questioned Farid and me about our trips to Delhi and Thailand; now, the train ride provided an opportunity for him to ask in detail.

We spoke softly in Farci, so as not to offend the few Indians in our car in hearing of our conversation.

"Tell me, Farid, about the Delhi people," Shah asked. "Where do most of them come from?"

"Most of the Delhi establishment are a mix of the Aryan tribes," Farid said.

"I understand they are a lot like we in origin?" said Shah.
"Yes, but most are Hindus. They make up the higher castes who dominate the northwest region of India, and are mainly Brahmins and Kshatriyas. They command the best of the religious, professional, military, and government positions in New Delhi. As we, they're people of Indo-European blood. They have light complexions similar to ours, with strong, pronounced features.

"They're generally taller than the rest of the total Indian population, excluding the Muslim Drogma tribes and some of the nomadic tribes along the far northeast border next to Afghanistan."

"Interesting." Shah wiped his forehead with his drenched handkerchief. "Damn, it's hot in here. Anyway, what about the shorter, dark Indians I see all the time in Peshawar?"

"Mainly Dravidian and other tribes of true local Indian descent. They were originally indigenous to the Central and Southern plains of India. They control most of the local retail trade and lower government positions in the city.

"These people possess an amazing, natural ability to withstand the scorching Indian summers here that take out the weak like a pestilence."

"I can definitely appreciate their tolerance to heat," Shah said, as he brushed his drenched hair away from his muddy forehead.

He paused, and pointed out the window to a line of wagons, pulled by water buffalo, heading in the same direction as we. I said, "Those families are probably going to Delhi too. Old Delhi is now a sea of refugees, mostly farmers, who left the parched countryside to work in the city to feed their starving families. Delhi's population is close to eight million now, with a third of them not having any permanent job or place to stay. They sleep on the street almost every night. They're called pavement dwellers. Shah, wait until tonight, you'll see. They fill the streets of Old Delhi every night."

"Yes, exactly," Farid said. "At the current rate of birth, the university scholars say the total population will be close to one billion by the year 2000—a third of them living in the cities. Imagine people walking around in never ending circles, an abortion of humanity."

"Incredible," Shah said. "Tell me something about the area we'll be seeing tonight."

"Sure, but let's move over to the seats across the way. I'm waddling in a pool of thick mud," said Farid.

Just then, the train stopped at a station. We pulled up to hundreds of Indians, many of them carrying their only possessions in life. I stuck my head outside my window to observe the madness. With the exception of the first-class cars, guarded by armed porters, the entire train was engulfed by passengers who pushed and shoved their way on board the already-crowded cars. The biggest and boldest won out. Some travelers, without children, climbed up the side ladders to ride atop. Entire families pulled back, to wait for the next train. Only one couple boarded our car.

Once again underway, we resumed our chat.

Farid spoke, "Shah, the hotel we'll stay at is located in one of the historic parts of Old Delhi. New Delhi, the southern section of the city and home of the capital, is like another world, with its magnificent English Raj architecture and manicured lawns, streets and gardens.

"Old Delhi has been re-built at least ten times in the last five to six hundred years. The gurus and sages of India have always spoken of Delhi as the city of changing faces. As soon as a conqueror took over the city, he rebuilt a new city over the older one, only to have a new conqueror take it over. To no avail, as the new ruler completed the city to his architectural tastes, it would again be taken away by force."

"Sounds futile, just as the efforts of the past invading armies who have tried to hold our country, but always failed," Shah mused. "Just as the Russians will find out."

"Yes," Farid chuckled. "And, during this century, the English are the prime examples of a senseless attempt to control Afghanistan and India.

"One example, in New Delhi, just as the British Raj added the final touches in completing the Presidential Palace: Rashtrapati Bhawan, the English Viceroy granted India's independence in one of the Palace's great halls. The Palace has been the home of India's prime ministers ever since."

"Poetic justice," Shah smiled.

*   *   *

When we finally disembarked, all four of us looked as if we'd just slept with swine. The mud had caked and stiffened the bottom of our jeans and backs of our shirts.

So much for first class travel on the Indian railroads.

We couldn't wait to get to our hotel in the city. When the cab let us off, we immediately flipped coins to see who got to take a quick bath first. The change of travel plans had put us easily five hours behind schedule, so we had to hurry.

I was second up, and the mud on the floor from Yosif's shower lay everywhere. Only two steps into the room, and the muck had already squished through my toes. The maid would have double duty. I gave her a handsome tip when I exited the shower room.

Our hotel was a classic example of an Old Delhi hotel: an antiquated, three-story building with the reception desk in the front entrance—which the proprietors had made into an inviting garden area. It teemed with lush, planted palms and flower beds.

We stayed in two large adjoining rooms on the third floor, with a common door in between. Yosif and Farid shared one room; Shah and I, the other. The facilities were clean and, in addition it provided us a secluded, central location for our activities for the evening.

We first had to meet Mr. Tara Singh, a Sikh travel agent with an office located in the upper New Delhi district, called Connaught Place. It bordered Old Delhi. Mr. Singh had our airline tickets and the necessary forged visas that would get us into Bangkok.

Connaught Place, a famous locale, and known for its colorful hodgepodge of respectable import-export and warehousing businesses, towered above a busy circular street that enclosed the park. Discount retail shopping outlets took up every inch of available space along the street. In recent years, a newer, underground mall had been built in the center of the park itself. A seedier element occupied the outer fringes of the business area. Here, illegal money-changers and drug dealers of heroin and opium reigned over the side streets.

The four of us went by taxi to Connaught Place. As we were leaving the hotel, Farid said, "Once we meet with Tara, Shah and I will not tarry. I've arranged to meet with my contact for Shah's passport. We'll be leaving by taxi right away, and you can stay on with Tara for dinner if you like. And afterward, we can all meet back at the hotel, later."

We all nodded in agreement.

Our driver, whom we tipped well to get us through the

crowded, smoggy streets, had great street driving skills, and we arrived in satisfactory time.

Mr. Singh's fourth-story office directly overlooked the park. We didn't need a doorbell to announce our arrival. We sounded like a slow procession of water buffaloes clamoring up the old wooden stairs to reach the third floor.

We made our way up the last flight, and Mr. Singh stood at the top, waiting. He rubbed his hands together, muttering, "Yes! Yes!"

"Gentlemen, welcome to India!" he proclaimed.

"It's so good to see you, Tara," replied Farid. "Thanks for your patience."

"No problem. I'm sorry you had to take the train during this time of year; it's a scorcher," Tara said. "Come into my office, I have great air conditioning."

The nine-by-twelve foot office felt like a walk-in refrigerator. A welcomed relief. The four of us sat down on a long divan right in front of his desk.

"Farid, your tickets and visas are all ready, per your instructions. Here, check them out." Mr. Singh leaned over his desk to hand them to Farid.

His bright, wide smile spread over a deep, dark brown face. His traditional Sikh beard came to a point, halfway down his chest—jet black against his pure-white muslin shirt and shorts.

"How was your taxi ride over here from the hotel?" Went well I take it?"

"Yes, everything went fine," Yosif said.

"The reason I asked is, this dreaded heat lately has everyone thinking crazy. The past few days, a lot of the beggars—the pavement dwellers—have been pestering the tourists and business people around the local neighborhoods surrounding the park."

"They usually do," Yosif said.

"Not like this. They've been mobbing people in rick-shaws and even taxis, desperately begging—even to the point where children lie down in front of cars, pretending to be dying. During the distraction, other youths sneak from behind the vehicles and steal ladies purses, small luggage, and such.

"The police are trying to stop it, but it's hard to control. It's been very upsetting to everyone here. There are traffic jams everywhere."

"Pray for a cool spell," I said.

"Everyone is doing just that." Mr. Singh said.

"The tickets and papers look perfect," Farid said.

"Good," said Mr. Singh. "There's a fine restaurant down-stairs below. You gentlemen must be famished. I'll buy."

"We could use a bite to eat." I rubbed my belly. "My stomach is arguing with me."

"You and Yosif can enjoy," Farid said. "Unfortunately, Shah and I need to go to meet someone. Do you mind?"

"Of course not! We'll dine the next time you're in town for business," Tara said, fondly.

As planned, Farid and Shah took off in a cab to meet Farid's contact six blocks away from our hotel. Shah looked forward to getting his first personal passport, already stamped with India's immigration entry stamp. We would all be set then for our nine-thirty flight to Bangkok in the morning.

After a quick dinner with Tara, Yosif and I took an old—Morris English cab. An autorickshaw, a rickshaw powered by a motor scooter, was definitely out of the question since I car-ried the jewels on my back.

The driver smoked a cheap Cheroot cigar, which

smelled sickeningly sweet.

"Would you mind putting that thing out," Yosif said. "The smog and dust outside are enough without that thing stinking up the car."

The driver's quick look in the rear view mirror at Yosif's intimidating frame and huge black eyes, must have impressed him. He quickly extinguished the cigar.

People jammed the streets. Every block or so, the neighborhoods changed. One minute we drove through a Hindu section, the next—a Muslim or Sikh neighborhood. On each street, the looks of the business and home fronts, the attire and grooming of the street merchants, the smells of the cooked foods, body odor, the sweat of animals, and burning incense were totally different than the block before.

It seemed as if it changed countries with a simple hop, skip, and jump in any given direction. A real circus.

"This is one of the most unusual, craziest cities I've ever visited," said Yosif. "Every time I come here, I just shake my head in total amazement."

"Me too," I replied. "It's like you say, this city is crazy. On my last trip here, I took a friend out for dinner one evening, and we took an autorickshaw since it was his first time in Delhi. That turned out to be a big mistake.

"We got caught in the middle of a small riot between the Hindus and the Muslims. Turns out, they fought over a small Buffalo calf that had wandered down a Muslim street and disappeared."

"Let me guess," Yosif said. "A starving Muslim family had hustled off the sacred calf, brought it home and butchered it."

"Exactly. It's food to them. We had to jump out of the rickshah, shove our way over to a fruit stand, jump underneath, and wait until the authorities arrived—one hour later.   Six Muslims were taken away, doused in gasoline, and set afire."

"Sick savages."

"They also killed three Hindus in the combat. Many on both sides were maimed. Total bullshit. Needless to say, my friend lost his appetite from what he saw, so we went straight back to our hotel, by cab. I haven't taken any rickshaws in these neighborhoods since."

"Wise."

About twenty minutes into our trip back, we came to a complete stop.   The taxicab driver threw his hands into the air and started to curse out his window.

Yosif and I stuck our heads out of our windows and craned our necks.   Directly in front of the cab, two large elephants stood face to face, decorated with colorful flowers and costume jewels. A girl, shrouded in beautiful silk robing, sat on top of one of the elephants. A young man in a gold suit, and wearing a huge turban that dwarfed his head, sat on the other.   A throng of people had huddled around, singing and chanting in Hindi.

"A wedding," we said to each other in unison.

"Appears to be a traditional one at that," I added.

"We may as well get out and walk through the procession, as to be stuck here in traffic," Yosif said. "Let's catch another taxi a few streets down. I'll walk right behind you and guard your backpack, as we squeeze through."

I paid the driver. Seemingly disgruntled by the loss of an anticipated longer fare, he mumbled off a few words to himself that I didn't even want to understand.

As we walked through the packed street, Yosif and I watched the guests sample food and drink from an ample array on tables placed outside several restaurants.   When we neared the end of the crowd, a plump, full-breasted woman came toward us, hugging the people around her, and chattering like an excited crow. Her advanced years and exquisite dress made me think she could be the mother-of-the-bride or groom. She finally reached us, and said, "Welcome. Welcome to our wedding party!" She bubbled over with enthusiasm. "We have enough food for many. Please join us in this great celebration."

I glanced over at Yosif who gently shook his head.

"No thank you," I said, although it is very kind of you to ask. We just had dinner. But please, give our best to the bride and groom."

As she walked away, Yosif said, "Probably an arranged marriage. Happens all the time in this part of the country. But at least they aren't children. They look to be in their early twenties."

"Yes, true," I replied. "It wasn't too long ago that it was still tradition for wedding ceremonies and futures to be decided for adolescents."

We arrived at our hotel twenty minutes later. Farid and Shah had not yet returned, so Yosif and I decided to play a game of cards. We sat down at a small table next to the window in my room. The window overlooked the street below, a single-story down.

As I sipped from my Pepsi, I could see the shadows of the macaques, India's sacred monkeys. They swung from the rooftops across the way and stopped from time to time to watch the excitement below. They waited until morsels of fruit fell to the wayside on the narrow street below, then scrambled down to retrieve them. The macaques went to sleep right after the last stalls closed around eleven o'clock at night. Thousands of them lived on the rooftops in the older, dilapidated sections of Old Delhi.

Shah and Farid came in about half past midnight.

"How did it go?" Yosif asked impatiently.

"Fine. My man hadn't left yet. I paid him his normal fee of four hundred and fifty dollars, for the passport."

"Did anybody follow you?" Yosif said.

"There were some groups of men roaming around us, but I don't think we were being followed," said Farid.

"Shah, what do you think?" I asked.

"Well, I had a funny feeling we might be under surveillance," Shah said. "But that could be attributed to my uneasiness of being in India for the first time. But I've been suspicious since I've been with the Mujahidin.

"Let's hope nobody is on to us," Yosif said. "We'll be out of here tomorrow morning, bright and early, to go over to Mr. Singh's office. We should try to get some sleep. Ready, Farid?"

Yosif and Farid started towards the door that adjoined our two rooms, when we heard three loud knocks on the door of their room.

Everyone froze.

Four louder knocks followed.

Yosif pulled his .45 Smith & Wesson from the back of his waist.

"Who is it?" he called out.

More pounding answered.

After a moment of silence, I heard a few low voices just outside the door. Then, the door handle twisted back and forth, as a knife blade came protruding through the doorjamb.

Yosif pointed to his gun, nodded his head to us, and whispered, "Go!"

He ran over to his door and fired three shots at the center of the door. Shah followed right behind Yosif's lead. He knelt just to the right side of Yosif, and cranked out several rounds from his .44 Magnum.

The loud report made my ears ring like hell, my eardrums shocked numb.

Farid and I drew our weapons.

"Get your backpack. I'll cover," Farid instructed as he aimed at the front door of our room.

I flew headfirst, underneath the side of my bed, and grabbed the pack with the jewels to put on my back.

The front of our door rocked from men trying to push through the threshold.

"Fuck you, Assholes," Farid yelled as he clipped off several rounds of his 9mm Luger.

"Run, Abdul, get out the window! We'll follow behind." With the backpack on, I ran to the table, shoved it away from the windowsill, and turned quickly around with my gun, prepared to shoot.

As my head turned to him, I heard an automatic firing. A line of bullets ripped through the door and tore straight through Farid's chest.

He dropped, weaving to the floor. Bright crimson blood pumped out from his wounds. His head rolled over to my direction. His eyes stared open. He lay still.

My God—They killed Farid!

"Farid, Farid! Damn you bastards, I'll kill you!"

The gunmen now shoved my door inwards, but the dead weight of Farid made it difficult for them to enter.

I plugged off four shots from my 9mm, then bolted back toward the window, and jumped over the sill to land on a wide ledge several feet below.

Yosif and Shah continued to yell. The booms and flashes of their firepower shook and illuminated the room's walls.

I turned toward the street. A crowd of people huddled below shouting, Jump! Jump!" But I couldn't do it.

A thin telephone pole, six feet from the ledge, proposed my only way of escape.

I quickly turned back around again, and squeezed off three more shots inside the window, and stashed the gun under my waistband.

When I faced the pole, it seemed like twelve feet away, instead of six. I felt queasy and my head seemed to float.

After a second of eternity, I leapt for my life, with my arms stretched out as far as they could go. My body dropped several feet before my hands found the telephone pole, and as I grabbed it, the flimsy pole lunged forward. I hugged it in desperation. The gun popped out of the back of my pants and fell to the ground below.

"Shit!"

The pole continued to bend fast under my weight, in the direction of the building across the way.

Damn it! Swing back so I can slide down.

It splintered, sending me straight away into a balcony, a story down, in front of glass doors. I landed backwards, just over the railing, without hitting the glass.

I looked over to our hotel and my room. Three large Indian men pushed and shoved to be the first through the window.

I turned around and tried to push the glass door open. It wouldn't give.

"Wait! Stop, don't try to run. We won't hurt you," a voice yelled from across the street.

Right!

I put my entire weight against the door. A bullet whizzed by and shattered the glass, as I fell head first into the room.

Screams of women greeted me inside. I looked up to see two butt-naked, young Indian women running outside the room's inside door. An older European man, forty years or so, lay frozen in the bed to my left, with a blank look on his face, hands high in the air.

Hell, I was in a whorehouse!

More automatic gunfire came from across the street. A hail of bullets splintered woodwork and shattered vases in the room.

The loud screams of the distressed monkeys above on the rooftops, mixed with the frantic cries of the half-dressed concubines who ran down the hallway in front of me.

I've got to get out of here.

I flew through the door into the hallway. The girls yelled out in English, "Don't kill me!"

"I'm not going to kill you. Get out of my way!"

I ran down the hall like a madman. The girls hit the floor. In a frenzy, I bolted down the stairs.

At the bottom of the flight, an Indian man confronted me. I kicked him in the groin, and he went down.

I busted through the front door in a blind run. A crowd of people met me.

"Get out of my way!"

A street vendor stupidly grabbed for my pack. I shoved his fingers backward and they made a loud, cracking sound. His cry startled the curious deadbeats who flocked around. I dashed through an opening in the crowd for my break into the street.

I looked up towards my window for my attackers. Gone.

Shit, they're on their way down. Damn, where in the hell are Shah and Yosif?

I raced down the street. People jumped out of my way.

At the next corner I turned and headed down a very dark, narrow passageway, only to be greeted by a complacent water buffalo chowing down on spoiled vegetable scraps thrown into a cement trash bin. He turned his head and snorted. There wasn't room for me to squeeze through.

"Move it, you beast!" I picked a wooden crate from the bin, threatening to strike.

He reared back out onto the main street to get out of my way.

The shrill of the Indian police's whistles infiltrated the air in every direction. I ran hard, down the dark path, and straight into a group of hollering monkeys on the street.

One macaque jumped onto my back and put a stranglehold around my neck. I ran towards the side of the street and cursed loudly, as I rammed him broadside against the stone wall. He screeched and dropped to the street.

"Fuck you, monkey bastard!"

About a hundred yards down, I could see a wide, well-lit street. I ran as fast as I could. My legs ached in horrific pain, making it a real effort to put one leg in front of the other.

Damn it, where am I going?

Finally, I rounded into the street. Quite a few people milled around the local shops, still open. I looked around to find some familiar landmark, but recognized nothing. After I caught my breath, I saw a merchant who was closing up his store, and asked for directions to Connaught Place. Fortunately, he understood my pigeon Hindi and pointed out the way.

I had some distance to go, but couldn't afford the risk of taking a taxi driven by a snitch. I ran like hell.

I finally stopped running, My legs had given out. I curled up in a small entryway on the side of the street. Police whistles shrilled in the dark night.

The gangsters were right on top of us, after all. Quite obviously, they had a lot more pull than any of us had ever figured. They had already killed Farid. What happened to Shah and Yosif?

I put my head in between my legs and broke into tears.

*   *   *

I rested for close to two hours before I made my way over to Tara's office. The only people left on the street were drug addicts and sellers. I jogged at a moderate pace—the best I could do—and, in the process, pushed two begging addicts out of my way. The last hour had forced my body past endurance, still fighting the injuries from my torture six months earlier.

In certain areas, I had to jump over pavement dwellers asleep in makeshift beds on jam-packed streets. In the midst of one jump, a young girl sprang up from her bed, taking me by surprise. It caused me to lose my balance and twist my ankle. I shouted out in pain. She shouted out in Hindi, "Please sir, money for my family?"

I hesitated, then decided to pull some coins out of my pocket, and hastily handed several to her. She stared back with big, brown, sad eyes. I quickly patted her head, before turning around to painfully limp off towards Connaught Place.

I finally arrived at the back side of Tara's office building at a quarter-past-five in the morning. The homeless had started to get up from their bedding. Street vendors positioned their carts into place, and stores opened their doors for business. Another day, another dollar, in this dense sea of humanity.

I could see nothing of Shah and Yosif, and when I tried the door to the back of the building, I found it locked. Almost forty-five minutes passed, before the front door on the park side of the building opened for the merchants and travel agents to start their day.

As I approached the door I saw Yosif and Shah coming from a row of trees across the street in the park.

My heart leaped. *Thank Allah, they're alive!*

We met and hugged, but no one said a word. Their pale complexion and long faces clearly showed their anguish. My stomach knotted.

We went in and headed for the fourth floor of the building. We wanted to fill Tara in on the tragedy. He could possibly be in harm's way. We waited for his arrival by the stairs.

"How did you guys get out of the rooms?" I asked.

"We propped up the bed mattress and continued to fire, until the police whistles scared them off," Yosif said.

"Yes, Dear Brother, I saw you crash through the balcony door across the way from our window. You were very lucky," Shah added.

"Any casualties on their side?" I asked.

"They paid—two dead by our door, one by yours," Yosif said sternly. "We figured there were six or seven of them that attacked us."

A few minutes later, Tara climbed up the stairs.

"Why so glum?" he said frowning.

"Our friend—your friend—Farid, was killed last night in a gunfight at our hotel."

"No, don't tell me this. It can't be! "By who? Why?"

"A gang of Indian men most likely hired by the thugs in Peshawar," said Yosif. "I'm so sorry," he said softly.

Tara stood silent for a moment, then, looking down at

the floor, said, "I know a cousin of Farid's who lives in New Delhi. He'll handle the arrangements. I'll take you to the airport first and then go to see him. Let's go. I'll drive my car round to the back exit. Wait for me inside the back door until I drive up."

We lay low in the back seat of Tara's car as he drove us to the terminal. The three of us looked at each other in painful silence.

When we arrived, Yosif said, "Thank you for all your help. Indeed, what happened to Farid is a great tragedy. Here are our guns. We aren't going to risk carrying weapons into Bangkok."

Tara looked at us each, squarely in the eyes, and said softly, "May your Allah help you."

As the plane left the ground for Thailand, I placed my hand on the empty seat next to me—Farid's.

CHAPTER 10

Hell in a Hand Basket

A throng of girlie pimps surrounded us as we descended down the plane's stairs at Bangkok's Don Muang airfield. Middle-aged men dressed in silk outfits shoved each other out of the way to display albums opened to nude, teenage girls—most of them looked like they couldn't be over seventeen or eighteen years old.

A younger, aggressive hustler, laced in gold necklaces, tried to get in front of me and stepped on my right foot—the one with the swollen ankle. Sharp pains shot all the way up my leg and back.

"Get off my feet! Get away from me."

"But Sir," he said gleefully and took a half step back into the crowd.

"I'm not interested," I shouted.

"But sir, I'll take you to your hotel for free, in my taxi, and pick you up later this afternoon with your friends. You can meet these beautiful girls, at no charge. They love men like you. You men like women, right?"

Yosif intervened, "He said he's not interested. Are you deaf?" He picked the lad up by the back of his collar and set him quickly aside.

The other touts got the message, and the pack of wolves backed off.

"They think every male passenger who gets off a plane is a damn sex manic," Yosif said.

I looked over and saw Shah's eyes and mouth agape.

"Did you see how young those girls were, and without a stitch on," he said.

"It's people like you they want to talk to," I said, with a slight smirk.

"Not me. The girls are too young, and I'm happily married. Besides, I'm dedicated to our faith."

Yosif and I looked at each other and laughed. It felt good. Farid would have appreciated the laugh.

"Let's pick up Stella at the hotel and take her to lunch," said Yosif. "I'm anxious to see what's happening on her end with my Korean associates."

After a relatively easy customs check due to Thailand's lax "honor" system, we caught a taxi just outside the main terminal. We arrived twenty minutes later at the Metropolitan Hotel located in the southern downtown river-bank area of Bangkok, close to the Satborn Bridge. Yosif told us that he and Stella had stayed there several times together on business trips.

The taxi's air conditioner blasted cold air, as did every other accommodation in the city. Without the blessings of Freon, the unbearable humidity would have taken its toll on foreigners and made it too hot to fornicate—not good for business in the renowned City of Love.

"I'll be right back," Yosif said. He jumped out of the cab and walked into the front, hotel lobby.

"It's a big man," said the driver.

Shah and I both nodded our heads and grinned.

He smiled back at us through the rearview mirror. He had immaculate, straight, snow-white teeth and bright, oval eyes—a familiar, genuinely friendly look of the people of Thailand.

On my one other visit to Bangkok, the locals had treated me very well. They will act respectfully and gladly help the tourist who shows courtesy in regards to their customs—especially their Buddhist shrines. But arriving in town as one of the hordes of foreigners after sex, will gain you the same respect as you'd expect from any whorehouse or casino in the world that accommodates you for a price. Like they used to say to the American soldiers who spent their R&R leave here during the Vietnam years, "Whatever you want, Joe."

In general, the Thai display tolerance for other cultures. Bangkok's Islamic Thai, converted three hundred years earlier from a conquering King, were allowed to meld into the general Buddhist population. Fortunately, they didn't have to face the same malicious discrimination that the Indian Hindus have shown towards other religions and races.

About five minutes after he walked into the hotel, Yosif came quickly out the front lobby doors. A Thai, whom I'd never seen before, kept close by his side.

Yosif opened the passenger's side door, jumped in, slammed the door shut, and proceeded to pound his fist on the top of the dash. The driver jumped straight up out of his seat. The Thai, a thin man dressed in all-white attire, down to his shoes, hastily got in the back seat right next to me. Small beads of perspiration dotted the top of his forehead.

"Driver, go around to the back street of the hotel— quickly," the Thai said in English. The driver nodded his head and accelerated fast, out into the street.

What the hell—is something wrong? Damn!

When we turned the corner to head to the back of the hotel, Yosif finally spoke, staring straight ahead. "This is Rocky, my so-called trusted contact here in town."

Rocky leaned over to Shah and me. "I'm a longtime friend of Yosif," he whispered. "There is a big problem with Stella, but it is not my fault. Yosif is extremely upset. We go now to my car around back so we can drive to where we can talk in private."

I looked back over at Shah. He rolled his eyes and threw both of his hands in the air as if to say, "Now what?"

After we left the taxi, everyone piled into Rocky's white Renault sedan. The tires squealed, as he pulled away from the curb.

"Slow down, Rocky," Yosif growled. "Let's go to the Lemon Grass, but don't draw any attention to us. O.K.?"

"Yes, yes," Rocky said nervously.

In silence, we drove several kilometers east of the hotel, to an out-of-the-way restaurant that Yosif and Rocky frequented on past occasions.

Once inside the Lemon Grass, an original traditional Thai house turned into a restaurant, Yosif chose a corner booth for us. We ordered tea and asked for menus.

"Rocky, tell them." said Yosif, as he massaged the back of his bulging neck.

We leaned forward.

"Stella called me from her room last night to say she was safely in," Rocky stuttered. "She told me she needed a good night's sleep and would go shopping downtown in the morning."

Rocky stopped to wipe beads of sweat away from his brow with his front-pocket handkerchief.

"I went to her room this morning, about thirty minutes before you arrived at the hotel. She didn't answer my knock, so I asked the front desk if there were any messages from her." Rocky wiped his brow again.

"Well?" Shah asked.

"The desk clerk gave me a note in an envelope addressed to 'Friends of Stella,' and I tucked it away. I went outside to the doorman to ask about her. He told me about a half a block away, he had seen the lady I described, waving to a private car that drove up to her. He said she then talked to two men, who had stepped out of the car to greet her, and several minutes later, she got into the car and they drove off. As soon as Yosif arrived in the lobby, I gave him the note to read."

Yosif handed me a piece of folded stationary and, with eyes afire said, "Read it to Shah."

I opened the paper to find a handwritten note scribbled in obscure English. I read to all at the table in a barely audible voice:

"We want part of what you got. You ever want see her again, phone this number tonight."

Shah and I sat speechless.

Yosif's knees lifted the table and slowly rocked it as a rolling tempest. His eyes glared right past me, into space.

The waiter arrived with the tea and menus, and Yosif lowered his knees, so the table settled down.

"Yosif, why don't I order for us what you and I had the last time we ate here? Remember the chicken dish? All will like it, I'm sure," Rocky said.

"Fine," Yosif said, no change in his tight composure.

"Do you know who the kidnappers are?" I asked Yosif.

"Not yet, but we will. It's my guess the bastards must know Stella and me to have plucked her away so easily as she left the hotel. We need to buy weapons right away. Rocky knows the right people. We can trust him. He isn't at fault for what happened to Stella. I did kind of take it out on you, Rocky, didn't I?"

"It's okay. If I'd showed up a little earlier and hung out in the lobby, I might have prevented this." he said.

"You didn't know this was going to happen," Yosif replied.

"Do you think Stella is okay?" asked Shah.

"Most likely," Yosif said. "As soon as we secure guns, we'll call the bastards and find out exactly how much of the jewels they want in exchange for her. If they even touch a hair on her head, I'll..." Yosif made a big fist and his face turned bright red.

"We'll get Stella out. We're behind you." I touched his bulging arm.

"Whatever it takes—whatever," Shah said.

When the meal finally arrived, hardly anyone ate a thing, though the food tasted good. My appetite had disappeared ever since Yosif and Rocky jumped into the taxi at the hotel with the bad news.

Rocky picked at his Roasted Lemon Chicken and rice with his chop sticks. He threw the food around his plate instead of eating—first from one side, then to the other. Finally, he stood up, and said, "I can't eat. I'm going to make a few phone calls about getting the weapons."

The next ten minutes, the rest of us resumed almost the same eating behavior as Rocky's earlier futile attempt. No one said much of anything—we just kept our heads down towards our plates.

To our relief, Rocky arrived back at the table with a cheery smile. "It's a go!" he said boastfully.

Yosif quickly threw some money on the table to cover the check, as the rest of us strode out of the restaurant. After all of us had piled in the Renault, Rocky hit the foot pedal, heading out towards the docks along the Chao Phraya River that runs through the heart of Bangkok.

"I called my elderly friend who always has a very good selection of guns and ammunition, at a fairly decent price," Rocky said. "He and his family live along the klongs, our interwater canals on the west side of the Chao Phraya.

"By the way Shah, you will see a totally different way of living out in the Klongs—not at all like the hard, Wali desert you're accustomed to in Afghanistan, my friend."

In less than thirty minutes, we boarded a private, *rua hang yao*—a fast, but noisy, narrow long-tailed boat, so nicknamed because of the long, propeller shaft that extends over the shallow transom which the driver hand-controls for speed and direction.

We all sat low in the vessel with our knees almost up to our chests.

After crossing the wide river, we headed down the narrow Klong Mon canal. The look and feel of Bangkok changed drastically within minutes, as if we had entered a cultural time warp to several hundred years earlier.

Shah turned his head slowly back and forth, panning like a Hollywood cinema-graphic camera. His eyes didn't blink. After several minutes of taking in the whole scene, he shouted out, his voice barely audible over the engine noise, "Amazing. Everyone here lives on the water, either in a boat or in a house built on stilts. There's not one single home on dry land. Simply amazing."

After Shah's comment no one said a word. Only the loud, high whine of the propeller's motor rang in our ears. This was no happy-go-lucky guided tour. We had a serious mission—Stella.

After fifteen minutes, we pulled up to a row of houses atop very high stilts. Each home had their own dock underneath.

Following Rocky's instructions, the driver tied up to a half-submerged floating dock. Four young boys quickly swam up to us from the neighboring house.

"Misters! Misters!"

The first boy to arrive hoisted himself up on the boat's edge, right next to Yosif.

With a big smile, he touted, "Look what we have here

for you—look!"

The boy pushed up on the bottom of a carved bamboo stick and out jumped a crude, stick man that popped an erect red penis.

"Look! You like?" the little salesman said with glee.

I had to smile a bit. Even Yosif let out a slight smile.

"Here, take this dollar. Now go!" Yosif said.

The boys swam off in laughter. Yosif stashed the toy down in between the seats.

Rocky told the driver to wait, and we got off the boat.

We gingerly ascended a short narrow flight of old stairs with very thin, recently-repaired worn steps, to the house above.

Several long clotheslines greeted us. They hung low to the floor with women's clothing, left out to dry.

"Follow me," said Rocky. "Do not go under or jump over the lines with woman's clothing. Do not touch them either—very bad for men. It takes away your personal aura and brings bad luck."

We walked completely around the clotheslines.

At the front door, a young man, maybe twenty years old, greeted Rocky. After several minutes of private conversation, the man went back into the house.

Rocky turned around to us.

"Everything is A-O.K.. Please take off your shoes and follow me into the house."

Three young girls, maybe nine or ten years old, welcomed us. Blushing and giggling, they immediately grabbed for Yosif's huge arms to lead him in the door.

"Thank you." Yosif smiled.

After settling us inside, the young, innocent vestal virgins ran out the front door, chattering like excited schoolgirls after the first day of school.

"Welcome to our home, Rocky and friends," announced a voice from the back of the house. An elderly man, wearing a black robe, appeared through the door. He wore a long, white goatee that fell about nine inches from his chin.

Rocky stepped forward. "This is your honorable host, Mr. Lai. He welcomes you to Bangkok!"

"Please come this way, gentlemen," he said, and disappeared into the back room.

We crept towards the dark room. I smelled an old, musty bamboo scent permeating the house. Flashes of the sun, reflected from the water below, broke through the loosely-fitted floorboards that creaked with every step we took.

In the back room, Rocky lifted a heavy burlap curtain that hung against the door and gestured for us to go in. In the middle of a small five-by-five room, Lai sat in a lotus position, with two young men, in excellent physical condition, seated on either side of him, Israeli Uzis laid upon their laps. Five 9mm handguns, two 38s, and two Ak-47s lay spread out on a large, embroidered, red silk cloth.

"Follow my lead," Rocky said to Shah in a low voice.

Rocky bowed forward, his hands placed flat together in a prayer directly under his chin. We respectfully did the same.

Lai and the two men followed us with the traditional *wai* greeting.

"Please sit down. Welcome to our home. These are my two sons, Chow and Chi," said Lai.

The young men, who showed no expression whatsoever on their faces, bowed their heads forward to us.

Rocky guided us. "Do not cross your legs. Either squat on your knees with your feet behind you, or sit with your legs and feet off to the side," he whispered.

"I understand you need some weapons for an emergency that has arisen," Lai said. "These are the only guns I have available now. Please inspect, as you choose."

"The 9mms look good," I said to Yosif who sat nearest to the weapons.

"Sounds fine to me," added Shah.

Yosif nodded his head in agreement. He took three of the handguns—two chrome Barettas and one Smith-and-Wesson—and briefly checked them for barrel condition and lever/cartridge performance. He nodded in approval to us.

"They look fine. How much with three boxes of rounds thrown in?" asked Yosif.

"Twelve hundred for three guns and ammunition," answered Lai in a cool, calm tone.

"Okay," said Yosif, as he reach into his tote bag and pulled out a wad of Ben Franklins. He counted off twelve, and placed the money on the cloth.

Lai turned to the son on his left and gave him a nod. Chow immediately hopped up and went to a small closet behind them, and returned with three boxes of ammunition—still in their original wrapping.

After a few courtesy exchanges, we excused ourselves and walked back down to the boat, three of us were armed and ready for whatever lay ahead for the evening.

"Are you hungry now? I bet all of you are. You hardly touched anything on your plates back at the restaurant," said Rocky, winking in jest.

"Look who's talking," said Yosif.

"Sure, We're all starved," Shah said.

"We'll pass plenty of boat food-vendors on our return, or we can get dropped off at the Oriental Hotel a few blocks from where we parked the car and grab a bite to eat at one of hotel's restaurants. There are plenty of phones in the lobby," said Rocky.

"The Oriental Hotel sounds perfect," Yosif said.

Rocky rattled off some words in Thai to the driver, who then throttled the motor to a deafening whine and we fishtailed away from the dock.

Once we got back on the Chao Phraya River, we headed south towards the Oriental Hotel's landing. The late-day sun cast an intense yellow glow over the downtown riverscape. I turned around and looked north to see the Grand Palace with its surrounding shrines gleaming a bright gold. The brightness cast a beautiful hue about its neighboring, twentieth-century skyscrapers. Soon, the bright neon signs of Patpong, Soi Cowboy, and Hana Plaza—the red light districts of naughty bars, live sex acts, and escort parlors—would shine as bright colorful sentinels in this town of many facets and faces.

As we got off, everyone thanked the driver for his expedient services. Rocky paid him handsomely, and we walked up to the hotel located on the embankment that overlooks the river. It felt good to enter the refreshing air-conditioned lobby. The Oriental's famous and lavishly-furnished hotel lobby boasted an 1800-vintage, grand, golden dome which topped off its imperial elegance. The finest hotel in Bangkok.

We walked into the Author's Lounge and sat down to order from an a la carte dinner menu that reflected some of the favorite dishes of famous authors who had stayed there.

After the four of us selected sandwiches to eat, along with savory Darjeeling tea, Yosif leaned in to speak.

"Since I'm very familiar with this town, and since this involves Stella, I'm going to make the phone call to these nappers, whoever they might be, Okay, Abdul? Shah?"

We nodded in agreement.

"Yosif, I would like to go along with you to stand by the phone and listen in," I said.

"Sure, let's go."

"Here are some local coins for the phone," Rocky said, handing Thai tokens to him.

Several vacant phones filled in a quiet corner of the sprawling lobby.

Yosif inserted the coins into the phone and dialed, the muscles in his face and throat rigid.

After Yosif heard the first words come over the receiver, he cupped the phone piece, and said, rather surprised, "They speak Farci, I know who they are."

They're speaking Farci! Who in the hell could it be—someone from our country?

After a minute of fast, heated conversation, Yosif took a piece of paper and pen from his front pocket and wrote down an address. He slammed down the receiver.

"Who was it?"

"Two chump, drug dealers in town that Rocky and I know. Their names are Johnny and Smiley. I recognized Johnny's voice on the phone. He sounded higher than a kite—on smack I think. I met the bums several times, through Rocky, to buy small amounts of cocaine and hashish for visiting clients of mine who buy jewels from me. Several of my customers like to entertain prostitutes in their hotel rooms at night during their stay. Nothing very serious."

"What do you mean by saying they're chumps, and how do they know Farci?"

"Several years ago, they used to be pretty big movers of drugs to Indian and Iranian dealers here, and in India. But, when they let their personal social habits get into their productivity, they were cut off from the big boys, and now they're both addicted to heroin.

"Anyway, their former business associates around town must have told them about our shoot-out in Delhi. That, or the boys in Peshawar called their contacts here. Nevertheless, somebody put the word out on us around town."

"How did they snatch Stella so easily?"

"These two jerks knew that Stella and I liked to stay at the Metropolitan when we're here in Bangkok for gem cutting and brokering. They had met her once or twice before, when they were there to drop off some drugs. So, its my guess that those punks put together what we were up to and staked out the hotel entrance this morning. They saw her come out, probably met her just outside the lobby, and offered her a friendly ride downtown to the shopping mall— only Stella didn't know their real intentions."

"Do they have the big guns behind them?"

"No, like I said, they're low-lifers now, with no organization at all. Last time I heard, they're roommates and barely make ends meet, because of their habit."

"How is Stella? What do they want?"

"From what I could tell, Stella is fine. I could hear her voice in the background, but that's it. She sounded upset, but her voice was clear. I don't think they drugged her."

"Good." I patted Yosif on his back.

"As far as the jewels are concerned, they want a third of what we have in our possession. They want us to bring all the jewels with us tomorrow morning, at seven o'clock, to their place—no cash. We need to catch them off guard, tonight. I'm going to make them pay for this stupid stunt. Let's go to the table and talk with Shah and Rocky."

Rocky's jaw dropped when he heard who had kidnapped

Stella. Shah showed surprise at two losers having the gall to try to pull off a job like this, especially with a bigger notorious gang from Peshawar, the hunters.

Rocky knew the location of the dope dealers' address— a gated apartment community on the edge of downtown, mostly used by small-time prostitutes.

After we finished our meal, we walked back to the car and headed straight to the red light district. We had to drive through a good portion of it, just to get to the dealers' apartment complex about eight blocks outside Patpong 2 Road.

The flashes of blazing neon lights, loud cackles of laughter, and blaring American hard rock music came through the opened doors of Patpong's carnal night spots. But no one paid any attention to the action on the streets, except for a few curious glances from Shah. We looked rather like a hearse full of morticians on the way to pick up another stiff. With the look in Yosif's dark, staring eyes, he became the Specter of Death, his cold, blue-steel Baretta in hand.

At ten o'clock we pulled up a block away from the front gate of the complex.

I handed the backpack to Shah and said to Yosif and Shah, "I'm the smallest one here, and Rocky knows the complex. We're going to get out, sneak through the gate when a car goes through, and survey the situation around their apartment."

"Okay," said Yosif as he looked over to Shah in agreement. "But, promise me you won't do anything until you come back and get me."

"Of course not. It never entered my mind."

"Good, we'll be waiting. Be very careful."

"Here, take my gun, Rocky. Go with Allah," Shah said.

Rocky and I walked casually down the street. As a car passed, we struck up a conversation. When we reached the gate, we positioned ourselves behind a thick bush, adjacent to the gate's opening.

"I know a couple of good-looking girls who live here," whispered Rocky, his eyes devilishly twinkling.

I gave a chuckle. "Good for you."

"The apartment should be somewhere to the left side of the entrance. When we get in, follow right behind me."

Within a few minutes, a car headed our way ready to leave the parking lot, and the gate opened. As the vehicle passed by, I could make out two, heavily made-up young women, rocking back and forth in their seats to their blasting stereo. We dodged into the complex before the gate closed.

We trotted around the side of a rather narrow, but oblong structure. The heavily-wooded grounds made a stealthy approach possible.

After a couple of guesses, Rocky found the right apartment. He and I made out a dimly-lit front living room, with a sliding glass door. A small bathroom, located right next to it, had the lights on. Every window appeared to be closed shut, and drapes drawn. I could see the silhouettes of a few people as they walked in and out of the bathroom.

"Maybe they're shooting up smack, big time, and they'll be defenseless to our surprise attack," I whispered.

Rocky gave me a big smile and nodded.

I looked around to find that behind the apartment, about twenty feet away, stood a five foot wall—not very high but with a thick hedge in front of it—and on the other side, beyond that, was the public street.

"I've seen everything I need to scope out for now. Let's go, Rocky."

We made it back to the car in less than five minutes.

As we trotted up, Yosif and Shah nervously tapped their

fingers on the car doors. I leaned over the passenger side window to confer with Yosif.

"Well, come on, what happened?" Yosif barked.

"What's the problem?" I said, upset with his tone of questioning.

"I'm sorry. I'm worried about Stella."

"It's okay. As far as we can tell, they seem to be milling about in the apartment. They have one window and a sliding glass door in the living room with the drapes drawn shut. The bedroom can't be seen. The bathroom's window—right next to living room—is not shaded, but it is so high up we can't tell what's happening. We did notice quite a few ceiling shadows of people walking in and out. We thought they might be cooking horse in there, but that's just a guess."

"Yes, yes," said Rocky. "It looks like both Johnny and Smiley are there, and maybe another person or two with them. Can't really tell though."

"What's the deal? Is it time to go in?" Shah asked.

"Of course," Yosif said.

"Let's do it," I said.

"I guess I'm staying with the jewels," Shah said.

"Thanks, my friend," Yosif said with a warm smile. "Be ready to hurry down the street with the car should we need you."

The three of us sneaked through the gate in the same way, and Yosif headed around the other side of the apartment to knock on the front door. He would give us two minutes to situate ourselves on the other side. Rocky and I, guns drawn, went right up to the living room windows to see if we could see through any small openings of the vertical blinds. They were shut tightly. We motioned to each other, confirming that neither one of us could see inside. Rocky put his ear to the smaller set of windows. I put mine against the sliding door.

I heard Yosif's loud knock at the front door, followed by silence. Then I heard Yosif arguing with another man. A young Thai woman started to yell inside the living room.

I need to know what's going on, damn it!

Rocky looked frozen in fear, like a doomed cow that knows its about to be shot right between the eyes.

"Rocky, come here," I said in a low, but urgent voice.

I'd never seen a man move so fast to get to my side.

"Let's go over to the bathroom window. Then, give me a boost so I can see what's going on."

He shook his head twice "No" but gulped out a "Yes."

"Let's do it, now," I said.

We scurried over to the bathroom window. He got on his hands and knees so I could climb on top of his slender, bony back.

Just as I was about to reach up to take hold of the bottom of the windowsill, all hell broke loose.

Someone came crashing through the sliding glass door to our left. The unexpected loud shatter of the glass caused Rocky to lose his balance. He collapsed and I went sprawling to the ground. I landed on my stomach in a dull thud.

"It's Johnny on the ground!" I heard Rocky yell out.

As I tried to regain my senses from the fall I saw Yosif come out of the broken, sliding glass door in a backward stride, clipping off a few rounds from his 9mm back towards the apartment.

Johnny started to rise back up.

"Look out behind you. Johnny is getting up," yelled Rocky.

Yosif quickly turned around and swiftly kicked Johnny in

the gut, screaming "Take that, you fucking bastard."

Then, Yosif turned around again and yelled, "Run, Stella, run!"

I heard Stella screech, "Get off of me, you filthy bitch."

Stella emerged from the door, and I could see every muscle in her body tighten in ripples as she ran.

"Damn it! Get me out of here," she cried.

Yosif clipped off two more rounds just to the right of her. A man screamed inside.

"I'll finish you the next time, you Scum Bags," Yosif yelled out in mocking laughter. "Let's go. Over the wall. Now!" He grabbed Stella's hand and they ran for the front-street wall.

I turned to see Rocky already in flight, going over the five-foot wall with the hedge in front of it.

Yosif jumped up and sat on top of the wall and pulled Stella up. Then they disappeared.

I stuck my gun in my back pocket and took a flying leap. My hands caught the top of the wall yet my strength failed to lift me over. It should have been a piece of cake, but I fell straight into the hedge.

I tried to lift myself over the wall once more, but my left leg got stuck in the thick foliage, and my sprained right ankle could not muster the strength to hoist by body up to clamber over the wall.

Forget your injuries, get over!

I heard the Thai woman yelling bloody curses behind me. Then two gunshots. Plaster shattered about by my head.

"Damn it!"

I struggled again to get my foot out of the bush when, suddenly, a huge hand grabbed mine from over the top of the other side. I flew over the wall like a rag doll and landed in

Yosif's arms.

"Having a little trouble, my dear little brother?" He laughed heartily.

We ran like hell towards the street. Shah pulled up the car to a screeching halt. We all piled in and Shah hit the accelerator.

"What happened?" Shah asked.

All but Rocky broke out in hysterical hoopla. Rocky had scooted down into the well of the back seat, still wide-eyed.

"Thanks guys!" said Stella, out of breath. "I thought I'd never be rescued from that rat hole."

"Well, what happened, damn it?" Shah asked again.

"As you can see, we're all here and safe. That's what happened." Yosif laughed in his grand manner.

"Shit, just another day at the races for you, Yosif!" I said.

"Hey, where's Farid?" Stella asked.

Our laughter turned to silence.

Stella looked over at Yosif, who stared straight ahead. Then, she looked to us in the back seat. Her stare caught my hopeless expression of futility and grief.

Tears filled her eyes.

"Yosif?"

Yosif looked down at her and put his arm tightly around her. "He didn't make it. He was shot down in a gun battle at our hotel in Delhi, last night."

Stella buried her face in his shoulder and bawled.

Yosif held her close. A tear fell down his cheek. Shah drove onward without a word. Dead silence filled the car.

We drove straight down Rama I Road for at least three miles. Shah darted in and out of lanes. We wanted to lose any possible tails from the apartment complex.

"Let's get out of the car as soon as we can and take a cab

over to the Hilton International," Yosif said. "Rocky, do you
know a perfect spot for us to get lost in the crowd?"

"Yes, Sir. Just two more blocks, straight ahead. There's
a major entertainment complex, complete with movie theaters, nice restaurants, and fashion stores—just like America.
Big crowds, too.

"I'll take over the wheel and you guys can high-tail it.
I'll head straight back to my pad. Too much action for Rocky
tonight. You know, you guys are really fuckin crazy."

As soon as we arrived at the intersection, we got out, and
Rocky jumped back behind the wheel.

Yosif slapped Rocky on the back. "I'll call you tomorrow,
after we are done with our business. You can tell me how
much we owe you for your splendid services and I'll have it
delivered to you."

"Great, but next time leave me out of John Wayne gun
fights. No fun for Rocky.

"Good luck, my friends. You'll need it," he smiled and
sped off, disappearing into Bangkok's madness.

"Sweet man, isn't he?" said Stella, with a hint of a smile.
"How did he take it when I disappeared? How did you take
it, Yosif?"

" We'll talk about it when we get out of this mess," said
Yosif, curtly, surveying the busy street.

"Sure you will—like you always do," Stella said with a
sly, but sweet smile.

Across the street stood an imposing entertainment complex. It had a marvelous-marble staircase, classy enough to
adorn any government's state building. It reminded me of
the U.S. Senate building steps in Washington.

The timing was perfect to disappear in the mall's foot
traffic. A large crowd emerged from one of the theaters. A

few Thai couples had enjoyed a night out on the town, but most of the couples were Thai call girls with their foreign dates from around the globe. They hugged and kissed like high school sweethearts. Because of the amount of people that poured down, we had to walk up the left side of the stairs to get to the upper plaza.

Once we reached the upper level, we stood by several large posters amongst a crowd of people inhaling their cigarettes like there was no tomorrow. One of the large posters advertised a Bruce Lee Kung-fu movie. The other sported a typical Asian romance movie with a picture of a lovely, westernized Thai woman made up like Bridget Bardot. She looked off into the distance with pursed, luscious red lips and seemed to longingly caress the top of her large bosom, seductively revealed in a low-cut evening dress. A tall man lingered in the background, carrying a gun. It reminded me of a modern, Asian version of an old Casablanca billboard.

Every one of those romance flicks are the same in Asia, especially Thailand. All feature the same type of woman, the same story line—only with a different ending. The movies appeal to thousands of young Thai women, who dream to ultimately fall in love with a wealthy man and travel the world.

"Everything seems fine now. How about taking a taxi over to the Hilton?" I said.

"Let's find a phone first," said Stella. "I need to call our client to apologize for being late and to tell them we're on our way."

"Perfect," Yosif said. "There's probably one in the restaurant along the backside of this mall."

We weaved our way to the back restaurants and Stella found a phone to make her call.

"They're waiting for us," she said, when she returned.

"All right, let's get the hell out of here. One more step to go," Shah said.

"You're telling me. I'm the one carrying them," I tiredly smiled.

CHAPTER 11

The Barter

*W*e arrived at the hotel a few minutes shy of midnight. Despite the hour, guests continued coming in and out of the lobby. The bar still served, and the local girlie tout still had his glassed-in store open for people to peruse at their leisure the albums of beautiful girls. When it comes to love and sex, there was nothing sacred in that city.

"Well, let's give Jack and his entourage a call to say we're down in the lobby," Stella said.

She looked relaxed now from her ordeal and I thought she was quite the woman. I could see why Yosif was fond of her. Good looks, polite manners, and tough as nails.

Yosif and Stella went over to the lobby phone to call Jack's people.

"Hey, Abdul," Shah said, "why don't you join me for a peek at the albums in the tout's store? Didn't really get a good look at them at the airport, and I'm a bit curious." Then his face reddened.

"You go ahead. I'll stand near the entrance so I can see when they're off the phone."

Shah walked into the store wearing a sheepish grin. I stayed just inside the door. I had seen the books before. He picked up an album and fumbled through the first few pages. Five minutes had passed when I spotted Stella and Yosif coming back towards us. I hailed Shah, and he dropped the book. We scurried out.

"Shah, you look like the cat that swallowed the canary," Stella said, as they approached us.

"We were just hanging out," he said hesitantly.

"Oh, I see," she winked.

Yosif and I chuckled.

"Well, it's all set gentlemen," Stella said. "They will be

down to get us in another ten minutes or so."

We sat four across on one of the lobby's expansive couches. It felt as if we sat on a cloud. A definite improvement over the rough conditions we'd endured over the past ten days.

This was one of the newer hotels in Bangkok, a favorite of the high-class business set. It reminded me of New York City, with its American architecture and Western decor. The registration desk, manned by Americans, posted clocks along the wall with the time zones of the major cities of the world.

Fifteen minutes later, the elevator spit out three large Koreans, almost the size of Yosif. They walked toward us in a somber, menacing gait.

"Those are Jack's bodyguards," Yosif said.

One look at these unsmiling thugs made me think twice about who this Jack guy really was. Could Yosif had dealings with the Korean mob or something?

We rose and Yosif extended his hand toward the leader of the trio. The Korean and Yosif shook firmly.

The Korean then let out a creepy smirk. His shoulders were massive, and he must have weighed at least two-hundred-and-fifty pounds.

"Pleazz forrow us to...room, err, yourrr spezial suite." The Korean spoke in broken English.

Without another word, the three hulks turned around and started towards the elevators.

"Let's go," Yosif said.

Stella went to his side.

No introductions came and I felt very uncomfortable. I didn't like the looks of those guys. I wondered if we'd ever come back down again.

Shah and I slowly followed the group. Shah's hesitant

look told me he shared my apprehension.

I stepped up to Yosif, and tapped him on the back.

"Yosif," I said. "I'm not comfortable with these guys. Why don't Shah and I stay behind? You can take the jewels up with you. We'll wait in the lobby until you call for us—when your business is completed—if it's all right with you."

Yosif studied my face, then Shah's, paused, and said, "Ah, I see. You're both nervous. Don't worry—these guys won't touch you. Their boss is a multi-millionaire and he has never played foul since I've known him."

I gave him a blank look.

"Trust me," he said. "I've been doing business with him for years. He's quite a funny guy, actually. You'll like him. Let's go, you two."

"I'm just a little shaken from the last few days on the road," I said.

Yosif smiled and gave me a reassuring pat on the shoulder.

I looked over to Shah and nodded a come on. All seven of us stepped into the elevator. We looked like sardines in a can. On the way up to the fourth floor, the whine of the elevator was the only sound I heard.

When we arrived at the door of our suite, the head Korean turned around and handed Yosif the key.

"Pleazz make yourrr...zelff at home," he stammered. "My name Big Stan. Jack and people down real zoon. Ta-ank you."

He gave us that big imitating grin of his again, said something quickly, in Korean, to his two counterparts who bowed their heads slightly in respect. The three of them left and walked towards the elevators down the hall. Big Stan definitely had command of his men.

"Interesting musclemen," I said.

"Don't worry, they don't mean any harm," Stella said.

"Okay, okay. Let's see the suite." Shah shuffled about as Yosif chuckled and opened the door.

Shah hurried in and then stood stupefied at his new surroundings. I followed right behind, and was immediately impressed.

A floor-to-ceiling picture window ran completely across the outside wall with a beautiful nighttime view of downtown Bangkok, about three kilometers to the west. The lavish, sprawling suite had a fifty-by-twenty-foot main living space with two seating areas housing couches and coffee tables, a long dining room table, a mahogany desk with executive chair, and plush white carpeting throughout.

We took a quick tour. There were two bedrooms at both ends. Right in the middle of the suite's main room, a spiral staircase led to a large, raised balcony. It encompassed an area furnished with two more couches, a leather reclining chair, an additional round conference table, and a wet bar with a well-stocked refrigerator.

Stella leaned casually over the rail of the balcony above and said, "Well, boys, I don't know about you, but I'm going to pour myself a strong drink,"

"Yes, dear, relax. You deserve it." Yosif smiled up to her.

"No kidding." She smiled back with a cute twist to her dimples.

We climbed up the stairs to join Stella.

After everyone had something cold to drink, we settled down in the comfortable furniture to view the city from above.

"Listen, people," said Yosif, taking a sip, "I'm glad that everyone made it through the bad scene tonight, especially Stella."

Stella's eyes began to water.

For a while, no one spoke,

Then, Yosif said softly, "Do you want to talk about it, Stella?"

She paused for a moment. "I left the hotel around nine o'clock this morning to take in a little shopping and perhaps stop by the U.S. Embassy to visit a girlfriend whom I'd met back in my graduate studies at Princeton.

I started to hail a cab when Johnny and Smiley pulled up in their car and greeted me. They said they were going my way uptown and would be glad to give me lift. As you probably know, Yosif and I had done some business with them so I thought, what the hell. That's exactly what happened—I stepped into hell."

"What did they do?" asked Shah.

"Johnny pulled a gun on me and said we were going to their place for a while, until Yosif and you guys got in town. They told me that we had something that should be shared with them too. I knew they meant the jewels—but I couldn't imagine how they found out. Anyway, I told them to fuck off, and Johnny threatened to shoot me up with heroin if I didn't shut up and behave myself."

"Bastards," Yosif said. "What happened at their condo?"

"They proceeded to get totally fucked up on smack and were arguing with each other the entire time. They kept threatening to shoot me up if you guys didn't call soon. Then, Yosif, after you called, they started to argue even more. They acted as if they were out of their minds."

"Who was the Thai woman?" asked Yosif.

"Some two-bit whore from Patpong who wanted to get high, in exchange for sex. Johnny and Smiley went into the bedroom with her for about five minutes, but came right back out. The bitch yelled, 'You two can't perform, your fault. You still get me high, now!' Those two losers were so out of it they couldn't get it up," Stella said with a slight laugh.

We joined in on the levity of the situation. She came around with that smile of hers.

"Anyway, Yosif stormed in about a half hour later. You know the rest, and I'd just as soon drop the matter right now."

"No problem, my dear. I'm just glad that you are okay now," said Yosif. "By the way, when Frank and his men come up, I want everyone to make sure not to mention anything about the gang in Peshawar; including what happened to Farid."

We nodded in agreement.

"I'm going to lie here on this comfortable couch for a while," Stella said.

"Good idea," said Yosif. "Gentleman, let's go downstairs and put the jewels on the dining table to review once more before they arrive."

"See you in a few, boys," Stella let out a long yawn.

*   *   *

A knock at our door came about thirty minutes later.

"I'll get it," said Yosif as he strode over, opened the door a crack, and then smiled.

In walked two of the bodyguards, followed by a robust, older man in his fifties, with white, thinning hair. He donned a well-tailored silk suit and tie. Right behind him followed four other smaller Koreans in normal business attire, with the final third bodyguard right behind.

"Jack, how are you my dear friend?" Yosif said. "Please come in. The place is marvelous. Like always, you have outdone yourself on accommodations."

"I'm feeling grand. How are you? Wait, what is this sparse growth on your face? I've always seen you neatly shaven. Becoming a bit of a Bohemian these days, are you?"

"No, not really. The battery on my shaver wore out last week, and we've been on the road for several days. It's starting to itch," Yosif said, stroking his face.

"Don't worry, I just happen to have an electric razor on me. Please use mine," said Jack, pulling out an electric shaver from his coat pocket. A big smile came over his wide face, and his rotund belly started to jiggle.

Jack's group busted out in a roar of laughter. Yosif's face turned red.

The rest of us joined in on Jack's teasing, with laughter. There was a change in intensity with this group. I let out a long sigh of relief. Shah was still a little edgy.

"Big Stan told me you needed a shave. I thought I would play a little joke on you. You like?" said Jack, his eyes almost shut from his laughter.

"Yes, you got me" Yosif responded with a slight smile—his face still a little red.

"Well, Yosif, take the shaver," said Stella with a smirk as she looked over the railing.

Yosif looked up to her and gave her a wide grin and shook his finger at her. "Women don't have to worry about beards when they're all tied up because of unforeseen circumstances, do they?" he said.

"Touché," she said as she blew him a kiss.

Shah and I both stifled our laughter as we looked at each other and smiled.

The Koreans never caught on to Yosif's innuendo.

Jack reached out and handed the razor to Yosif who accepted with a nod of thanks and put it in his pocket.

"I'll shave later tonight. Thanks again," Yosif said, kindly.

"Come on up boys and have a drink. The bar is open," Stella said.

The bodyguards had a hard time going up the narrow winding staircase, but we all made it up and then sat around the conference table. Stella poured drinks for our guests, while Yosif laid out the jewels for their overall inspection. Jack examined the jewels and then pointed out particular gems for each of his four jewelers to inspect for clarity, color, and their ability to be cut.

The levity we had shared earlier turned serious again. Shah and I stayed out of all conversations, and spent most of our time downstairs, relieved to stay out of negotiations we knew nothing about. Occasionally, I would walk upstairs to observe firsthand how the business worked, but otherwise, we put our complete trust in Yosif. This was his field of experience. His call.

About three-thirty in the morning, Yosif gathered all four of us together in the master bedroom downstairs to tell us where we stood.

"They want to purchase a little over half of what we have. They're not interested in the larger rubies and a few other large stones. But, I have a client in Frankfurt who prefers the larger stones, and will pay a fairly good price, especially for the large rubies still encased in original riverbed rock. I've got Jack up to one million, two-hundred thousand for the selected stones. The remaining jewels can bring close to eight hundred grand in Germany. I think we should sell the gems at this agreed-upon price."

Shah nodded. "If that's the best offer you can get, then let's go for it,"

"Wonderful," Stella chimed in.

"I'll make the deal with them, then. We'll have Jack's people wire the money to our Swiss account, when the banks open later today. After we verify the deposit, the jewels are theirs," Yosif said.

"Fantastic," I said, with a big smile.

"Let's go up and shake on the deal, then," Yosif said and raised one arm high, making a fist in salute.

After final formalities, the Koreans left at four o'clock in the morning. Completely exhausted, my eyelids drooped almost shut—I could see them shutter down to black.

Shah and I shared one bedroom with twin beds. Yosif and Stella took the master bedroom. I called room service to have them wake us at ten o'clock. Five hours sleep would do us a world of good. I went out as soon as my head hit the pillow. The ring of the wake-up call seemed as if a moment later.

We hung out the entire day ordering excellent food from room service and having our laundry done. We slept off and on. The Koreans had reserved our suite for another evening. It felt good to relax, safely tucked away in the finest of accommodations.

About two-thirty in the afternoon, I received a call from our bank. The money had been wired.

"It went through. The money is ours," I said.

Everyone let out a hoot.

We looked like a room of Cheshire cats.

"I'll call Jack and let him know," Stella said.

Yosif, Shah, and I gathered to gaze out of the window.

"Well, Abdul, Shah, it's been a hell of a ride," Yosif said candidly.

"A lot more trouble than I think that any of us ever imagined," I replied.

"You can say that again," said Shah. "I told you you were

out of your mind that night back at the Green Hotel when you laid this whole escapade out to me."

"I told you so, I told you so." I mimicked Shah.

"I didn't say that, you did," he retorted with a smile.

"Hey, guys," interrupted Yosif. "Nobody guessed the jerks had that much pull outside of Pakistan. If we had, we would have done things a lot differently, or maybe, not at all."

"Knowing how pigheaded Abdul is, we still would have gone for it, no matter the odds," Shah teased. "There was no way you were going to give the jewels back, right, Abdul?"

"No way in hell. Not after what happened to me at the fort. Not a chance—no way," I said. "Maybe ten or twenty years from now, we'll shake our heads in amazement. I'll always feel guilt over Farid's death every day of my life."

"Abdul, he took the same chance as everyone here," said Yosif. "He loved the action—always."

"Yes, I know. I need to call Tara and see if Farid's cousin took care of everything," I said.

"Of course, my friend," Shah said. "Stella should be off the phone any minute."

I started up the staircase as Stella skipped down.

"Everything is done. Jack's bodyguards are on the way down to pick up their catch and will arrive within the half hour," she said, eyes aglow.

"Stella, thank you very much for everything. You've been quite the trooper through this whole thing," I said.

"My pleasure. Thank you for saving my ass," she responded with a cute wink.

"You're a great friend. I think you're the first woman to ever tame Yosif," I said.

"And what makes you think so? He has a mind of his own."

"Most certainly, and Yosif has known a lot of women but

he's never been so taken by one as he has with you."

"Thank you for such a great compliment. I care a lot for him as well—as I'm sure you can tell."

I sat down behind the bar on a stool, poured myself a cold drink, and dialed long distance to Tara Singh in Delhi.

Tara answered the phone after one ring. "Good morning, may I help you?" he said in English.

"Tara, this is Abdul. I called to see if you contacted Farid's cousin for arrangements," I said solemnly.

"Abdul, it's you. Thank God you called—Farid is alive!"

Tears filled my eyes.

"Yes?" I cried out.

"He's in intensive care, but the doctor said he's going to make it without any long-term complications. I just saw him this morning. He couldn't talk because he had tubes in his mouth, but Farid recognized me, and he smiled."

"Thank Allah!" I cried out loud. "This is unbelievable. I saw the bullets rip right through his chest!"

"It's a miracle. I know. But, the doctor said, the bullets missed all his vital organs and spine. He's a very fortunate man. Abdul, I'm so happy you called. Is everything okay there?"

"Yes, everything is fine." I laughed and sobbed.

Yosif, Shah, and Stella came flying up the stairs.

"What's going on?" Yosif asked.

"Farid is alive. He's alive!"

Shouts and cries of happiness filled the room to a full crescendo.

Yosif gave me a big, bear hug. The phone dropped to the bar counter with a bang.

"Tara is still on the line," I said.

Shah picked up the phone and chattered like an excited parrot. "Tara, it's me, Shah. Farid is alive? How is he doing?

What's his condition? Is he conscious—can he talk?"

We huddled around the bar, arm in arm.

A solid knock at the door came just as Shah got off the line with Tara.

"It's them," Stella surmised.

"I'll get the door. Let's go downstairs," Yosif said.

Big Stan came to retrieve the jewels.

"Evv-ree-one happy?" he asked with a large smile.

"Yes, very happy," said Yosif in his great jovial way. He looked over and winked at us.

"I tell Jack," Big Stan said

"Yes, please," said Stella, her eyes sparkling like diamonds.

"Ride to airport to-mmo-rrow?" Big Stan said.

"Yes, please," Yosif said, as he handed the jewels over in a velvet bag.

"Ta-ank you," said Big Stan.

"Tomorrow, then."

Yosif and Stan gave each other a hardy handshake. Big Stan left, closing the door firmly shut behind him.

That evening the lights of the city shone brightly. We ordered a beautiful dinner that filled our dining room table. Smiles and laughter greeted the evening.

At last, I had a pleasant night's sleep. The first in two weeks.

CHAPTER 12

The Toll of Frankfurt

*A*fter breakfast, Yosif called Jack's room to thank him for the business and for the first-class accommodations.

Stan and one other bodyguard waited for us in the lobby as we checked out, and then they drove us straight to the airport. Though Yosif and I had always enjoyed Bangkok, this was one trip we hoped to forget.

After an easy customs check, we boarded on the plane, and the flight took off on time. All of our hard times on this endeavor were past. We had only to sell the remaining larger stones in Frankfurt, and I would be back on my way to Laila.

Our flight took us straight into Karachi International airport. Shah would leave us now. We got off together to change planes and stood at the entrance gate to say our farewells.

"I'll never forget this trip," stated Shah. "I've been close to death a few times in the mountains, but never experienced anything like this before. I can't wait to get back to my own type of warfare. The Mujahidin needs me."

"You're a little homesick, as well," Yosif said

"Yes, very much." Shah smiled.

"Shah, I'll miss you and the Jehad," I said.

"You might miss me, but I'm sure you won't miss this insane war," Shah said, winking at me.

"Good luck in Afghanistan. Kick some ass." Yosif gave Shah a huge hug. "You were a great asset to all of us the last week."

"I'll miss you, you big brute," said Shah.

"Oh, he's just a big teddy bear," said Stella.

"That too," laughed Shah.

"Yosif, thanks for handling the jewels in Bangkok. I wish you luck with your client in Frankfurt."

"Thank you. Abdul or I will be calling you sometime

next week in Peshawar to let you know of the final amount to be split between us, okay?" Yosif said with a big shrug.

"I trust you guys, without question."

"Well, Dear, we are going to miss you terribly," said Stella, as she kissed him lightly on the cheek. "I hope to see you in a couple of weeks around town in Peshawar. Take care of yourself, and teach those Soviets a lesson for me."

"It will be my pleasure," Shah said.

"Do you think you'll be using your new passport anytime soon?" I asked with a straight face.

"Not for a very long time." He smiled as he turned around to leave us for his connecting flight.

"Go with Allah, brother," I said.

"I will," he said as he waved to us one last time.

We watched him until he disappeared from view into the next terminal annex.

I would really miss Shah. I could only hope Allah would give him the strength to fight on, and to know right from wrong in this unfortunate war. It was not a holy war anymore—a true Jehad. I had no regrets taking the jewels for ourselves. We deserved it.

Within two hours we had settled into our seats, on our way to Frankfurt—no glitches or questions at customs this time. I settled back to long naps in between meals. Yosif and Stella leaned in close to each other. It was pure heaven to see the two lovebirds relaxed and enjoying themselves.

When the wheels touched down, all three of us put our hands together, and smiled.

We made it, thank God.

The terminal teemed with determined travelers. Yosif led the way, grinning back at Stella and me.

"We are going to have such a beautiful time here," said

Yosif. "But first, I need to make a quick trip to Hanz's office to drop off the jewels for safekeeping until tomorrow's important negotiations. Then, this evening, we'll dine at my favorite of favorites."

We cleared customs in a breeze, Stella and Yosif arm-in-arm. Only Europe and the United States allowed for a Muslim man to show some public affection to a woman. They melded together. I thought of Laila and of soon holding her.

No more crazy adventures.

From the airport, we took the train straight into the Main Station in downtown Frankfurt. We arrived close to five o'clock in the afternoon. The hurried crowds reminded me of Grand Central Station in Manhattan at the height of rush hour.

When we reached street level outside the station, Yosif first needed to drop off the remaining jewels at his client's office situated directly across the thoroughfare from where we stood. He carried a large, black briefcase.

"Stay here. There are plenty of shops around to keep you occupied. Abdul, there's a nice clock shop several doors down. Take a Cuckoo Clock home to Laila. I should be gone no more than ten to fifteen minutes. I'll find you."

"Be careful, Dear," Stella said.

"Always, My Lovely."

"Listen, Abdul, when I get back, we'll catch a taxi to the Ritter Hotel. The place has fine accommodations within a very classic Renaissance building. Its front facade is beautiful." Yosif blew Stella a kiss and walked down the flight of stairs of the pedestrian tunnel that goes to the other side of the busy thoroughfare.

We finally saw him emerge on the opposite sidewalk. Yosif walked forward in a long stride. He was several buildings from his client's main, tower front lobby entrance. He looked great—a man definitely at the top of his game.

A trolley car passed, blocking our view for a few seconds.

"We're almost there," Stella said.

"I'll buy dinner."

"He won't let you," she said, laughing.

The trolley car passed by, revealing a small crowd around the spot where we last saw Yosif. My eyes looked back and forth for him.

Where is he?

Screams came from the crowd.

My stomach dropped.

"Let's go," I yelled, grabbing her hand tightly.

"What's wrong, Abdul? What's wrong?"

"I don't know. Let's go through the underpass. Quick!"

We struggled up the tunnel's stairs on the other side and swung around to find the crowd larger than before. Several women cradled their children to them, off to the side of the circle of onlookers.

We broke through the people to find Yosif, lying face up, in a dark pool of his own blood. Eyes open, he stared at the sky.

"No. No, my Dear God. Yosif! No!"

Stella screamed.

"Yosif, don't leave me now," Stella cried out. "I love you, you crazy man. Yosif, talk to me!"

Stella fell upon him. She grasped his chest, and laid her head against his.

"Yosif, don't go," she said. "What have they done to you, my love. Please don't leave me, Yosif. My God, don't leave me now!"

She embraced his lifeless body. Ten or more stab

wounds covered his torso—his briefcase gone.

"Yosif, wake up! Yosif, we're here," I said as I knelt down beside them.

He didn't move—unresponsive to our cries.

Bright red blood covered Stella's hands and had splattered the front of her blouse.

I slowly pulled her away from him.

"Stella, we have to go. The police will be here any moment. Come, we must go now. Please, Stella."

I got her to rise. She buried her head into my arms and shivered from her uncontrollable cries of despair.

The people in the crowd stared. No one blinked.

"He's dead," they said. "He's dead."

*   *   *

The next day, the newspapers listed eyewitness accounts that stated two big, unidentified German men stabbed a large Afghan man multiple times with long-bladed knives, and robbed him of his briefcase.

Yosif was well-known in the business district as a jewel trader who carried precious stones most of the time. From what I could surmise, somebody tipped off the wrong crowd in Frankfurt about his arrival yesterday.

Stella stayed in her room all day and called me once to say she would be leaving the next day to go back to Peshawar. She could hardly talk.

When I went to see her the next morning to say goodbye, the heavy makeup could not hide her puffy eyes.

She muttered her last words to me, before I helped her into the taxi for the airport. "Call me in several weeks at the Green Hotel."

Before I boarded my plane to New York that afternoon, I made arrangements for distribution of the Bangkok money over the next several weeks. The task took every ounce of personal fortitude I could muster up.

As the plane ascended into the clouds over Frankfurt, I placed my hand on the empty seat next to me. The personal price of the jewels had been too high. I turned my head inward against the window and cried in silence.

Laila, I'm coming home.